I0738305

HEY YOU.
WHAT ABOUT ME,

Bria Twon?

HEY YOU.
WHAT ABOUT ME,

Bria Twon?

EARTHA GATLIN

AHTRAE
PUBLISHING LLC

Hey You. What About Me, Bria Twon?

Copyright © 2020 by Eartha Gatlin

Cover image courtesy of Shutterstock. Cover design by Victoria Davies (Twitter: @VC_BookCovers).

Print book: 978-0-578-70183-7
Library of Congress Control Number (LCCN): 2021909642

This is a work of fiction. Names, characters, places, and incidents either are products of the author's imagination or are used fictitiously. Any resemblance to actual events, locales, or persons, living or dead, is entirely coincidental.

All rights reserved. Without limiting the rights under copyright reserved above, no part of this publication may be reproduced, stored in or introduced into a retrieval system, or transmitted, in any form or by any means (electronic, mechanical, photocopying, recording or otherwise), without the prior written permission of the author. The scanning, uploading, and distribution of this book via the internet or via any other means without the permission of the author is illegal and punishable by law.

www.therealearthagatlin.com

Dedication

Always for, Demond, Paris, Jasmine, Jada, JaKobe, and London,
my heartbeats forever and ever.

Author's Note

This is a work of fiction solely based on the writer's imagination. Any reference to actual persons, places, or things is purely coincidental and is intended for the development of a good storyline.

Acknowledgments

I am grateful to God, who has done exceedingly and abundantly more than I could ask or think, for giving me this gift. I thank Him for loving me in spite of myself, having patience with me while I took the time to figure out my life's plan and purpose, and most importantly for never giving up on me and never leaving me throughout my journey.

I hope this work inspires you while humorously entertaining you. My intent is to share some relatable experiences to all who are open minded and transparent enough to see themselves through the lens of my characters. As always, I write inspirational fiction with the desire to encourage you to be a better you as it helps me be a better me.

Thank you to my family for encouraging me to write and follow my dream. Thank you to my editor and new friend Chandra Sparks Splond for your professionalism, without you this work would not be done properly.

Thank you to my sister circle of friends, I appreciate you and know that you all are some of the strongest women I know, (you put up with me) I admire and respect you all deeply.

Oh and one more...just because she calls me her role model, here's to you Rach! I'm inspired to know someone thinks of me as such, I'm humbled.

...When God wants to get your attention, He throws pebbles, when you don't listen, He throws a brick.
—Oprah Winfrey

Chapter One

I WAS DRIVING, LISTENING TO sounds of Chaka Khan's
"Ain't Nobody." I was giddy as all get out and as excited as a kid
on Christmas Eve. I could barely contain my enthusiasm. I always anticipated my visits with Beaumont Jackson—Beau was
what he was called by his colleagues and friends. Fav was the
name I had affectionately given him , though I never called him
that to his face. It was short for Favorite. He was indeed my favorite guy. I had conjured up the term of endearment as it related to how special he was to me. I knew it was corny as hell.
So what?

So, here I was on a sporadic drive to see Fav after I had previously told myself the last time we were together it would be

just that, the last time. I was done. I guess I forgot to give him the memo. But somehow my body always vetoed my mind's vote to say no, and off to races I would go. Except I knew what I was going to was nothing comparable to a race. it was more like a sensual slow dance, one to which I couldn't wait to get in sync.

"Girl, you're getting too old for this," I told myself as I chuckled alone in my black Volvo XC90. "One more for the road." I rolled my eyes, threw my head back, and felt the warmth building up in my body. I must have been going through my Fav vexed transformation while attempting not to sound like some sex-crazed psychopath, of course trying to convince myself I wasn't crazy as hell.

The truth of the matter was since my divorce, I sort of liked not having to answer to anyone. I came and went as I pleased. I was fortunate to have a pretty good nest egg and was self-sufficient, so it was nice not having to rely on anyone or deal with relationship drama. My only vice—guilty pleasure, if you will—was my magnetic draw to Fav's beck and call or more precise, text to see him. I had been intrigued by him the day I met him. Who knew I'd be on the other end of a booty call at fifty-seven years old?

To keep things at a minimum, I never called Fav outside of our secret rendezvous. Who needed that complication? I certainly didn't, even though on occasion I found myself thinking about him daily, constantly. Truth be told, I could probably count on one hand the days I didn't think of him versus when I did. I couldn't recall a day when he hadn't crossed my mind. I wasn't hooked though, at least that was my rationale. I just had a lot of free time to think. Like an addict on crack, meth, or whatever drug of choice there was, Fav was my addiction.

Hey, don't judge me. I was a functioning addict. I mean, I didn't just sit around and wait on him. I did things. I had a full social life, I was involved socially, I was outgoing, took care of myself, exercised, ate right, and well, most of the time, a real social butterfly, if you will. I mean, people looked up to me, so how much better could it get, right?

Hmmmph. You can't tell people everything. They don't need to know your vulnerabilities, your weaknesses, your vices, so I kept some stuff to my damn self.

Hell, no other man sent me to the moon like Beaumont Jackson did. We fit together like chicken wings and hot sauce, coconut on a German chocolate cake, a banana on a split, a pea in a pod. Now I don't know if the feeling was mutual, but it sure felt like it when we were together, and to me that was enough.

Fav was very attentive, passionate, and extremely good at lovemaking, which is what kept me coming back to the tune of two-and-a-half years of being dick-notized, meaning I was whipped and in a complete trance or so it seemed.

Hell, men did this sort of thing all the time, so what if I chose to get mine from someone whom I enjoyed and who seemed to enjoy me as much. I was single, unattached, and so was he—at least that's what he told me—so my actions were justified. I had sense enough to know every relationship brings with it from time to time some strange dynamics, and this one was no different. We were simply two consenting adults coming together to fulfill our needs. Our relationship was a no-strings-attached, no-holds-barred, no-labels-needed encounter between a couple of chemistry-attracted heterosexual human beings.

I accepted it for what it was, and so for the time being, it was cool. I knew I didn't want it to end, so we made it work, no drama. It was everything I needed and wanted, at least for now. When it was time to depart, I already longed to see him again when only time again will tell. I was thinking should I phone him, text him, reach out to him... No. I would wait until next time. The only problem was who knew when the next time would be.

Of course I ignored the red flags. Why? Because I didn't want to not see him again, at least not yet. There was always very few words exchanged between us as it related to talking about building a tangible relationship. It's funny, although it was never actually said, that was not a topic up for discussion. In fact, most of our conversations were superficial. We talked about work stuff or random chitchatting pertaining to whatever was on the TV. I didn't care. All I knew was Fav had a way of making me feel like I was the only woman in his world when I was with him. I was passed gone. Fav's masculinity, even for a man in his mid-fifties, never left me unfulfilled. His affection encapsulated me and kept me wanting more every time. His lovemaking skills were incomparable to anyone I have ever been with. I couldn't wait to get to Fav.

When I finally got to my destination, I had all but dropped both my bags on the floor in the hotel room after entering the space when Fav embraced and held me for what seemed to last for hours. The warmth of his body was succulent—his soft, warm lips soothing touching mine; his breathing heat exuded to the opening of my mouth... His tongue met mine. Our tongues kissing, circling softly, tongue lovemaking, methodical tongue love-making, stroking together, rhythmically like a rehearsed dance, but this one hadn't been practiced, only anticipated. I literally thought my knees were weak. I thought there might be an awkwardness being with Fav after so long. But no, Fav was smooth. There were no words—only embracing, warm bodies touching, lips, and tongues touching. Fav stroked my hands. He lightly touched my fingers. I always enjoyed his meticulous touch, *It's the little things a girl likes,* I thought. Fav was always true to form. He never missed a beat. I wonder what he'd think if he could read my mind.

Fav was barefoot. Something about a man making love barefoot. I loved the idea of our bodies touching every single area from top to bottom, kind of makes you think he's into you as much as you're into him. Oh well, morning would come soon enough, so for now, I'll embrace this time.

Chapter Two

BY THE TIME MORNING CAME, I could already hear the birds chirping outside the window. Fav was still sleeping as I lay on my side of the bed waiting and hoping to have morning sex. Typically, it went like this: We cuddled, there was foreplay, more sex, then we both reached our fulfillment. Fav would get up to retrieve towels for me, then he'd vacate the bedroom. I knew that was my cue to get up, take my shower, get my things on, and prepare to leave. On a weekday, I was always out of Fav's by 6 a.m. On the weekend we slept in, and I was typically out of there before 9 a.m. I was cool with our arrangement. Like I said, it gave me the freedom to get some good, unattached companionship without all the strings attached.

I was riding in my car on my way home, my mind drifting back and forth as I reminisced about the evening, but not too much. I knew it would be a while before I heard from Fav again. I had grown accustomed to his pattern and being in the present when we were together, and when we weren't, I went on with life as usual. That was my choice in the matter. I accepted it and didn't demand any more than that. I guess our relationship was a lot like Carrie and Mr. Big's from the TV series Sex and the City .

Truth be told, my mind was ready to move on, and my sabbatical from being exclusive with a man had been long overdue. Every time I'd reach a point of no return, I would hear from him again, and again, and again. I felt like the kid who got to stay up late with the parent who had weekend visits. Once it was time to go back home, I had to get reacclimated into the routine. I was back on an emotional roller coaster and had to get my mind back right. It was too much, and I knew it was time to cut my losses and end my infatuation and seemingly one-sided affair with Fav. I had allowed it to get the best of me. I was obsessed with him, and my common sense told me I had to strategize a way to overcome it. But I also had come to the realization I didn't have the willpower to do it cold turkey. I kept telling myself if he doesn't text me again, cool, I'm good with it. I'm not reaching out to him either, and time will pass and bam, we're all good. No harm, no foul. The good times will be over, and I'll cherish the memories and move on. To make matters even worse, I guess it didn't help I hadn't really met anyone else worthwhile. I mean, there was no one who I was even remotely interested in.

I knew I had to do something to get over this fixation. The more in control I thought I was separating my affection for Fav, the deeper I sank. I was losing myself. I was becoming too vulnerable. I couldn't do that. It was just too much.

"You have to let him go." The words were as clear as a bell to me as I spoke them out loud. "This is insane, Sabria Twon. You've got to get a hold of yourself. Ain't nobody that damn good. Enough's enough."

It's as if I drive the highway in a fog, but thank goodness I made it home in one piece. As I pulled into the parking garage of my condo, I can barely see through the tears welled in my eyes. I touched the sun visor for the garage door opener, and simultaneously that was the moment of my epiphany. My mind was opened with the opening of that garage. It was like the door had opened, and aha, I knew it was time to do something different. I couldn't get out of my car and into the sanctuary of my home fast enough. For some reason unbeknownst to me at the time, I knew once I got into my private domain—into the comfort of my own setting—alone with my thoughts, the woman in the mirror, my secret place, that a life-changing experience was awaiting me. I came to the realization if I were to get something real, someone meaningful that I needed to release my past for once and not look back. As tough as it had been to let Fav go, he had that good-good love as one of my girlfriends had joked, so I knew I had been hooked, yet good common sense was telling me enough was enough, and it was time to move forward.

What I needed more than anything right now was to get him out of my system and reclaim myself. I wasn't running away. I was moving into a new future.

Chapter Three

I HAD ALWAYS TRIED TO be logical and practical as it related to making decisions—or so I thought. As with any goal, I needed to develop a sound plan of how to get there. I created a list with two columns with specific pros and cons. Financially, logistically, demographically speaking, I researched the cost of living, culture, climate, taxes. I didn't factor in jobs so much since I had no intention of finding other employment—at least not in the traditional sense. Neither did I consider schools because my children were adults.

Top of my list was a warmer climate. I was drawn to Dallas/Fort Worth, Texas, metroplex. For one, I wanted to be someplace where it was hot—I mean really hot. I loved climate change, but I thrived in sunlight and warm temperatures. I had on occasion visited a sister friend who had relocated to Dallas several years prior. I visited her and fell in love with the area, although she didn't live right in the heart of Dallas. She was in close proximity to Dallas, Fort Worth, Arlington, and several other places that seemed to have an appeal to me. Culturally, Texas sounded like a good spot for retirees. The cost of living, taxes, and I liked the fact that it was large enough yet small enough in the surrounding cities that I could fit in Plus, I enjoyed the southern hospitality.

I was especially drawn to the flowering redbud trees and their vibrant pink color, the succulent plants, as well as the high number of palm trees in the area. It reminded me of God's natural beauty all around me and gave me a sense of peace and tranquility. Driving at night, I was impressed by the lighted Dallas skyline on the architectural structures of the Omni, Reunion Tower, Bank of America Plaza, and other places in downtown Dallas. I thought it was something to see, especially how the lights changed depending on certain holidays and other observances. I was enthralled driving across the Margaret Hunt Hill Bridge for the first time. I could see the impressive white structure from a distance. Coming from a small town, seeing something so expansive ahead of me as I drove alone in my vehicle was a little bit intimidating. To say it was culture shock for me was an understatement.

But I welcomed the change nonetheless, and I was looking forward to bigger and better. I was ready to do something radically different for a change. Even if it meant me venturing out alone, leaving my adult children to fend for themselves...well, it was about time. Lord knows I had been Ms. Superhero Mom for the past few decades of my life. I was long overdue for a change—and I mean a change from everything and everybody.

Hey, and the best part about it was there were no state taxes on my retirement, so that did it for me. They say everything is bigger and better in Texas. Who knows, maybe a bigger, better Fav would find me 'cause this time around I'm not looking for him—at least not yet.

I think next time I'll opt for a more meaningful relation-ship—let's get to know each first, no sex. Hmmm, well at least it sounds good. We'll see. Meanwhile, there was so much to do. My mind was racing. I'm out of here. My first step, I called a realtor to put my house on the market. That was bittersweet. We had a lot of memories in my home, but oh well, as my momma would say, "All good things must come to an end," and this was one of those times.

I felt it was time for a change in scenery. There were times I would drive in my car going from point A to point B when I just wanted to floor the gas pedal to get the hell out of there. I just wasn't feeling it anymore. I couldn't seem to put my finger on it, but I just felt my time in Rockford, Illinois, was done. I was ready to go. I was tired of seeing the same old familiar sur-roundings. I felt that same thing when I knew it was time for me to retire. I got that same feeling when I knew it was time for me to end whatever relationship I was in at whatever time. I guess you can say I was paying attention to the pebbles God threw for whatever reason for me. I knew it was time to make a move. I had to go, otherwise I was going to die a slow, uneventful death with dreams buried, life unfulfilled, and regret, all of which was not me. Not at this stage of the game.

I had lived in shame in the past. I was no longer that person seeking belonging or trying to please. I was ready to do me as they say now. I don't care what anybody says, I'm moving forward with open arms ready to take life by the horns on to my next chapter, and I couldn't wait.

Next, I phoned my company's benefits administration line to see how money I had in my 401(k) account because in all practicality, I knew it was going to take some mullah to make this move, and being the sensible, careful person I am, I was ready to move, but I knew it had to be done decent and in order. Remember my momma, Bea, didn't raise no fool. I already had an idea, but I had created an Excel spreadsheet with line items to input the estimates for my move, so I needed to be exact. Next, I searched the Internet for relocating companies. I put in the estimated date of my move and was surprised so many options were available. It was almost overwhelming. Then I found a site that let me enter my zip code, projected date, email address then it responded with four or five relocating companies. Basically, there were so many movers to choose from, some would pack your stuff for you, others offered the option of dropping off those you-pack-and- ship containers. In other words, I could go full-service moving or do it myself. Just deciding on the aspect of how to move was mind boggling but I stayed the course and weighed my options based on factors, such as cost, who I could get to help me, and minimizing my stress, which was why I ended up choosing the full-service mover. I knew once I started the whole relocating process, I had to keep going. I wasn't going to talk myself out of moving ahead nor would I share any of my plans until I had all my ducks in a row.

Making my plans for my new journey became so exciting for me. When my thirty-six-year- old middle daughter India came by and saw the for-sale sign in the yard, she told her siblings, thirty-year-old Shea and forty-one-year-old Zach, "Mom, is going through a midlife crisis. She's not going to move."

India was somewhat misguided because based on our past discussions, I had indicated a desire to relocate to one of the Chicago suburbs. I had always loved Chicago the city and still do. But the drive from my hometown to the city was an hour-and-a-half drive one way. The distance from a suburb of Chicago to the city is a twenty- to thirty-minute drive. Instead, I'm sure India thought I would have chosen to move closer to Chicago because she knew how much I admired it. In the past, I often drove from Rockford to the city for shopping, dining, or just to drive along Lake Shore Drive because the view of the lakefront gave me peace and quiet. I simply enjoyed my trips alone. But since I'd grown older, driving to the city during the brutal winters had begun to wear and tear on me, particularly the snow and cold temperatures.

I understood why my decision had been hard for her to accept or even fathom. So yeah, to have made that choice, in India's mind, would have made more sense . Yes, we always talked about my moving to the Chicago suburbs, and as much as I disliked the woulda, shoulda, couldas, maybe I should have done it when I was younger, but I didn't then. The timing hadn't been right. Besides, I had a right to change my mind.

"But Texas? Where did that idea come from?" I later heard that statement from Shea, who from way back had always divulged family secrets. Shea told me India's exact words were, "Oh yeah, she done fell and bumped her head. She ain't going nowhere."

Even when I started selling my belongings out of the house and putting my family room furniture, dining room set, plants, armoires, and other home goods on that Facebook selling page, she still didn't believe it. I didn't care. That didn't stop me. I had made a decision and was working my plan to get on with my new life.

I supposed reality hit for my adult children after they received the group text I sent them detailing my plans along with the actual date I was scheduled to depart. Next thing you know, India and my small circle of friends, which ended of being about twenty-five guests, surprised me with a going away dinner party. I guess they knew then this old girl wasn't playing any games, and each day, my fear of the unknown turned into excitement the closer I got to my departure date. Relocation at my age was a major step. I felt I was finally doing something for me for a change. I was anxious to see what lay ahead.

I chuckle to myself as I look back on it. There was something I would often say to my children over and over, and that was, time flies even when you're doing nothing, so you might as well find yourself doing something constructive, put one foot in front of the other to reach your goals and before you know it, right before your eyes, you look up and bam, you have achieved it. Like so many other things I had decided to do in my life, once I made a conscience effort to do something, I didn't pay attention to anything or anyone around me. I knew what it was I wanted to do and remained focused and stuck to it. Who would've ever thought I would relocate at such an age? I surely didn't. But once I decided to do it and why I wanted to, I became desperate and eager to get there and take the necessary steps to put my life on a new path. I was tired of merely existing.

I had become stagnant. I felt like I was dying on the inside, not really living. My children were grown, I had been through two marriages and divorced. I had retired from a thirty-four-year career at ConEd 's nuclear plant. I traveled, yet I still felt disconnected. All things considered, I was in awe at how much time had passed. It's like you wake up and you're in a new place but in actuality each day brought me closer to my new destination. A few days had turned into several months.

Funny to think it had been six months since that move took place. I am loving my new hometown and have adjusted fairly well. Yeah, it took some time and a few wrong turns on the freeway to get the hang of driving in Texas, but for the most part, I had adjusted. I had even started to familiarize myself by taking the streets versus the freeway.

Now, with everything and everywhere, there are some cons. One thing I had to get used to was the traffic. It didn't take me long to figure out I had to plan what time I needed to be at my destination and factor traffic and the time it took to get anywhere. Being in a new town, I wanted to be safe. I wasn't willing to compromise that for the cost of where I lived, so I paid a little more for rent, but it was worth it. My condo complex was well groomed and manicured.

It had been several years since I hadn't owned my own property, but I loved the convenience of not having to deal with the cost of maintenance. Besides, I was just getting my feet wet. I wanted to get a feel for the new environment before I locked myself into a home ownership commitment. But that didn't stop me from going to tons and tons of open houses, and yes, it's true. Everything is bigger and better in Texas. I have seen some phenomenal houses. So I wouldn't become overwhelmed, I decided to just take my time, embrace where I was.

India, Shea, and Zach visited for Thanksgiving and Christmas the first year, and I popped into Rockford for very short weekend visits, so we were still all very much connected. As far as other immediate family connections, that was the extent of it for me because most of my immediate family was deceased, like my mother, father, and a couple of siblings other than an older sister. We communicated occasionally via phone and Facebook Messenger. Time certainly wasn't on our side as it related to living.

I had this sudden realization on life, a very real epiphany the more I witnessed the inevitable had occurred with so many of my loved ones. That's when my mindset started to change. In life, you're faced with many obstacles—mistakes you can overcome. You get another chance, a do-over, but with death, it's a wrap. That's it. There are no do-overs. You can't exit stage right and come back. That's when I decided I had some tough decisions to make and to figure out what was next for me.

My friend circle included my three girlfriends Harmony Jones, Sunetha Reynolds, and Connie Dunn. Harmony was my long-time ride-or-die from way back in the day. As it turned out, Harmony had met then married her husband, Jamal Jones, when she was forty-two. It was like a fairytale union. Harm had been swept off her feet. Jamal was a great guy, and they were happily married going on over fourteen years . Harmony had relocated with Jamal, and they resided in Winston-Salem, North Carolina. Ironically, Harm and Jamal had the same last name, but we checked and they were no relation. They had a grown folks romantic getaway wedding on the Costa Rican Islands. I was so happy for Harm. Although Jamal and Harm had surpassed the seven year itch theory, it seemed like yesterday they met and fell in love because every time we were around those two lovebirds, they acted as if they were still honeymooning.

Her husband doted on her very being. He was emotionally and materially stable, and from the looks of it, very supportive. He actually helped raise her two girls who turned out to be very fine adult ladies, and together they had a blended family of five adult children. All in all, life had turned out well for Harm, and I was very happy for her. We still maintained a very close long-distance friendship. Jamal would often joke he would see Harm tomorrow, whenever we got on the phone together because he knew we could go on for hours at a time talking. Jamal had to be a special man, one who was secure with himself and our relationship to accept our friendship. I adored him for that.

Harm and I had become real close with Sunetha Reynolds whom we all called Suni after meeting her at our church several years ago. Suni was in her mid-sixties. She was chic, very outgoing, loved to travel, and was very forward thinking about life in general, but she could be a bit irascible as it related to men and relationships, which, in my opinion, could be one of the reasons for her many short-lived courtships. No judgment, I'm just saying. Still, I loved being around Suni. She was hilarious and had a quick and natural way with words and at times an outrageous perspective on life in general. Suni could pray and cuss in the same sentence, which exemplified a realness I could relate to from my upbringing with my mother, Bea. Suni didn't have a problem vocalizing her opinion about anything at any given time.

Harm and I met Connie from the same church years ago as well. Back then, she was the church's director of Youth of Today Council with which we all volunteered. I recalled how back in the day our personalities would clash sometimes because of our ideas, and boy, we had some knockout disagreements, but at the end of the day, our goals were the same, so we learned how to overcome our differences and worked together to achieve what needed to get done for the youth. As it turns out, that's how it had been with our friendship. We knew how to be friends with one another. There was no mess and no drama.

We made a pact never to dog one another's children, which was a major deal. We first and foremost didn't dog each other, but definitely not the children. They were off limits. That was our agreement. Generally, when we got together, we solved most of life's issues—politically, religiously, economically, and socially. But more important than that, we were there for one another—family drama, whatever, it didn't matter. We had a safe, judge-free circle, but that didn't mean we gave each other passes when one of us was wrong about something. No, we called it out to whomever it involved and moved on.

It was Connie who incorporated our biannual girls trips. Connie was in her mid-sixties and married to her high school sweetheart, Chad. She was like the mother of the group, always setting us straight about politics, world news, and the importance of making sure we made time for each other even though we were all miles apart.

She and her husband relocated to Charlotte, North Carolina, because of his business. Connie and her husband were loaded in dough . Chad was a self-made entrepreneur who built a sizeable fortune by investing in stocks, bonds, and mutual funds. Since Connie didn't really need to work, she spent most her time planning trips so much so that she eventually started an online travel agency. We called her our girls trip travel agent. Connie always made sure we got five-star hotel accommodations whenever we traveled.

I was glad to have found a well rounded circle of ladies to be not only my girlfriends but who were supportive, loving, and wasn't afraid to tell you about yourself when you were wrong. These ladies were had been therapeutic in my overall well-being and vice versa, we had all been there for one another. As I reflected on our relationship, it reminded me of a card I read once that said, "every girl needs a nice pair of shoes and a good set of girlfriends to help 'em when they're down" and I don't know about anyone else but that always worked for me. I think it was because we had established boundaries carly on in our interpersonal bond, which had in turn set the ground rules for our everlasting friendship.

Out of the four of us, Harmony and Connie had been away from Rockford the longest. Suni still resided there, and I had been the last to relocate. Harmony was the youngest of our group, next it was me, then Suni. Connie was the eldest. Two married, one divorced, and one single. All of us had children and some grandchildren on whom we often doted. We laughed at and chided ourselves for how we had in the past allowed the grandchildren privileges not given to our own children. I especially loved to boast about my twenty-one-year-old granddaughter Zora. She was my pride and joy. It was hard to believe I wasn't happy when India became a teenage mom, but who could deny the love of a child who came into the world no matter how?

I would lovingly tease my girlfriends when we traveled at their purses filled with the "small medicine cabinets" they each carried along on our trips. I think most of them were on regular medications, like high blood pressure medicine and whatever. I was the only one I knew of not on a regular prescribed medication other than my glaucoma eye drops. Yes, I had been diagnosed with glaucoma in my early fifties. I recalled looking at the doctor like he was crazy when he said it. Then again, he must have looked at me even crazier when I asked him whether he thought I was too young to have the disease in the first place. That could have been the reason he didn't even respond. Oh well, I digress.

Before choosing Texas as my new home, the only other place I would have considered moving to was Martha's Vineyard. I loved it there, mainly because it's picturesque with the ocean and mountainlike views. Might I add that I absolutely adore most places with sand, a beach, and the ocean? The drawback was it's not the best in proximity to dry land. Being that I was moving alone, I didn't want to stress my family out to that degree by having to take a ferry or a small cropper plane to visit me. Naw, that probably wouldn't have gone over too well. India for sure would've said I'd lost my mind. Ha.

Moving was the breath of fresh air I needed. I most definitely had a deep appreciation for being in a new environment, going to and exploring new places on my own. Even if it was a quick run to Tom Thumb, Whole Foods, T.J.Maxx, the Highlands, Galleria Mall, or a show, the things to do and see were limitless.

Chapter Four

AS TIME GREW, I WAS living life as a retiree. My days consisted of early morning walks, weather permitting. Three times a week, I went to the fitness gym. Occasionally, I would meet a friend of Connie's to whom I was introduced prior to my move for dinner and drinks. The atmosphere was cozy and inviting and not too threatening, so sometimes I would stop in Gloria's Latin Cuisine alone for one of their infamous top shelf margaritas during the mid-afternoon hour. I was trying to adapt in my new environment and feel comfortable. Texas was large, but I didn't want it to feel formidable.

It hadn't taken me as long as I'd imagined to adjust. Like I said before, time had gone by so fast, I had been in the DFW arca since July, and by October I had attended the book signing of a home girl from Rockford. At this particular event, there was complimentary wine served, and as I observed the crowd, some of us had had a few too many of the plastic glasses of pinot or merlot, and you could tell because they seemed so engrossed in simultaneous conversations about purpose and fulfilling your dreams.

As I mingled through the network of females at the event, I overheard one of the ladies discussing a business opportunity that sounded interesting, and from what I had heard about alpha female personality types, she must have been the alpha female in that small group. I noticed the ladies surrounding her had their feet pointed in her direction, which from what I read was a sure tell sign they were impressed with her presentation. I enjoyed people watching. It was just interesting to see how people interacted with one another. I had been to so many net-working social events during my career that I wasn't interested in the overly impressionable types of folks at these kinds of events any longer. I could care less about that. I was there in support of the author. The rest of that nonsense was, in my opinion, for the birds. Although, I will admit, I do like to be inspired at times, and continuous self-improvement, growth, and development were high on my list of things to do, but this wasn't that.

The one thing I said to myself when I relocated was I didn't come here to be ordinary. I was looking to do something different. I always had an entrepreneurial spirit in me as it was indicative in the failed men's shoe store I'd set out to start in Rockford back in the nineties. I went so far as to acquire a business name, a tax identification number , researched where and how to get inventory, and then got stumped or better yet overwhelmed with all the legalities and information as it pertained to writing and submitting a business plan, and performing a market analysis. I learned there was so much more involved in opening a storefront when I met with the City of Rockford economic development representative. He gave me a few leads. One was the name of his sister who already had an apparel shop. Anyhow, the point is, my store never got off the ground. Again, the timing just wasn't right for me. I had to raise my family then and knew I didn't have the time it took nor was I willing to sacrifice my financial resources to gamble with a dream of that nature.

My second stint at entrepreneurship followed a few years later when I met a couple girls in my call center position at the electric company who worked on event decorating while taking calls. I became so intrigued by the cute little party favors, floral décor, and balloons that I went as far as to research becoming a party planner and balloon decorator. I learned the start-up was low cost financially, and it had the potential to reap really huge profit, so off to the races I went. For several years, I managed to operate an event planning and balloon decorating business, but like anything, I only got out of it what I put into it. I was too fearful to quit my day job, so in retrospect my so-called business was more of a hobby since I didn't make that much from it, although, I had quite a few events, weddings, birthday parties, graduations, and baby showers that I decorated. In fact, up until the time shortly before my move to Texas, I still decorated small events for family and close friends who would ask me to do it because they knew I put my all into it.

So, I guess it was not mere happenstance when I became acquainted with Isla Gray, Mona Porter, and Maysa Carr at Gloria's one late afternoon. I had stopped in to have one of the infamous margaritas and was minding my own business sitting at the bar surfing Instagram. Fast forward, the ladies and I ended up chatting and getting to know one another. Turns out they were there to discuss their current business venture, but after noticing me sitting alone, they decided to invite me over to have dinner and drinks with them.

Over the course of the time spent, it was like we had known one another for years. I learned Isla, a young astute lady, was a go-getter and way ahead of her time. Isla had married her childhood sweetheart, and together they had one daughter. Isla owned and operated Diva's, a custom apparel shop. She propositioned her besties, Mona and Maysa, and proposed the idea of opening a beauty bar at the same location as her custom apparel shop as a way to expand their businesses. Mona was an esthetician and Maysa a cosmetologist. Both ladies had furthered their education and gotten instructor's licenses, but weren't eager to teach in the industry, yet they were looking for some other opportunities in the field where they could apply their knowledge and expand their own individual businesses so they were readily open to the concept.

Mona was in her early forties and was married to an investment banker. They had a blended family of four children in college. Maysa who was in her forties was the single one in the group. She was seeing a guy she referred to as Todd Jerk-ins, and I later found out his last name was Jenkins.

Isla explained their concept was developed as a one-stop beauty experience for women. The ladies further expounded on how they all at one time or another had struggled paying rent at separate structures. They decided to find a solution to that problem by combining all of their services.

I loved it. These young ladies today have so much courage and enthusiasm, though it's funny to me, I now consider the forties as young. I was energized just listening to their story. I also learned these ladies took a chance, stepped out on faith, and one day decided to quit the beauty industry to become bosses in the field and follow their dreams. They came up with the idea of opening a beauty bar based on the concept of one-stop shopping for today's woman on the go.

Being the skeptic that I am sometimes—well, more times than not—I couldn't wait to see the spot for myself. I was curious as to whether their place was as good as they made it sound. So, when they invited me out to take a look around and offered me a complimentary spa service, I welcomed the opportunity and headed on out to their Waxahachie business. I must say I was quite impressed to say the least. I was immediately drawn to small-town feel of Waxahachie, which for me was about a thirty-minute drive south on Interstate 35 East.

I took my exit, continued down a long stretch of road a bit before I saw the narrow streets and a Victorian architecture. My navigation directed me to turn left, then right then right again, and my destination was on the right-hand side. I looked for the address when I saw a couple of ladies coming out of a corner door to the street. Coincidentally, I saw the sign, a large elegant D for Diva's, and I knew I was there.

All the parking places on the street were taken, so I had to go down a block and circle to get the spot one of women left open, which happened to be near the front entrance. I couldn't wait to get inside, judging from what I could see from the curb appeal of the quaint building, which housed three businesses—Diva's Apparel, Chic Hair and Makeover Salon, and Isla's Tranquility Spa.

I parked, went up to the door, and was greeted by a small foyer opening to three doors—to the right was Diva's, the center archway had a sign that indicated Chic Hair and Makeover Salon was up the beautiful staircase, and to the left was another opening that led to Isla's Tranquility Spa. Once in, I was already welcomed by the smells of jasmine and other soothing fragrances. I also had a sense of relaxation because of the sound of water, which I saw was coming from the small rock waterfall mixture of smooth black sandstone and white pebbles encased in a wall. The décor in what must have been the waiting area consisted of earth tones and neutrals. There was elegant oversized furniture with large pillows that looked like you were at home cuddling on a Saturday afternoon with a glass of wine. There were displays of skin care products for cleansing, serums, moisturizers, too many to become acquainted with at one time. Some of which I had no idea existed, like some of the face masks, exfoliating creams, toners, and body butters. Luckily for me, my skin had been good to me over the years. Genetically speaking, that was one good thing I was grateful my late mother, Bea, had passed on to me. Anyhow, the products were strategically placed and grouped by brand and color coordinated for guests to sample and purchase. Overall, the scent from the diffuser created a soothing ambiance, which made me feel very tranquil and re-laxed.

Just as I was about to take out my phone and give Maysa a call to let her know I was there since Maysa said the doors might be locked when I arrived, I heard a voice behind me.

"Hey, Ms. Bria. I see you made it. How was your drive out here?" It was Maysa.

"Not bad. Wow. I'm very impressed with your place. You ladies have surpassed my expectations. Great job. I can't wait to see the rest of the shop. Where are Isla and Mona?" I asked.

"I think both of them are with appointments, but they knew you were coming and are expecting to see you before you leave. I'll show you around the place," Maysa said.

On the other side of Diva's was the tranquility spa, an up-scale full-beauty spa owned and operated by Mona who was an esthetician who specialized in body treatments, facials, waxing, brows, lashes, and permanent makeup. On the upper level was Chic Hair Salon, owned and operated by Maysa, who offered full services in hair, nails, and makeovers. These ladies had worked hard and had set themselves apart from being just your regular run-of-the-mill traditional spot for hair, nails, pedicures, facials, clothes, and the like. They each employed a small staff to ensure their clientele received the best care possible.

We got done with the walkthrough then we ended upstairs in the hair salon area.

"So, from the looks of this place, I would venture to say you ladies are enjoying the fruits of your labor. It's fabulous. What a charming town. Waxahachie huh…I would've never thought to drive out here. This is a really nice location. I'm so inspired by you ladies the more I see and get to know you all. It's nice to see Black women who are friends working together. Your spot is amazing, and how awesome that you all agreed to follow your idea and put it together. Any regrets?" I said to Maysa as she poured us each a glass of white wine.

"I know, isn't it? It's like this spot was made just for us. It's so perfect, it's amazing what a little faith and a lot of hard work can do. The only regret I have is not taking the risk sooner. I think fear is the one thing that holds a lot of us back. I've worked so long in the hair industry and have seen how the times have changed. I just got to thinking me and the girls ought to do something together in order to keep our businesses afloat. We just had to get for real one day and decide we'd like to take a chance at putting a plan in place to coincide with the minds of today's sophisticated lady. And what better movement than to create what we felt like was a one-stop shopping experience for those bosslike and wanna-be boss women on the go, you know, like we sort of discussed the other night at Gloria's. We wanted to institute personalized services with a focus on the overall ex-perience. Here, women can relax, socialize, sip on a glass of wine, alcoholic or non-alcoholic cocktail, bottled water, or whatever theme drink the ladies choose paired with whatever mood suits them. You know today, Ms. Bria, women want the experience, not just the product or service. It's the experience that separates one establishment from the other."

"Well, I think y'all are on to something. I wish I had had this boldness back when I was the age you ladies are now. You girls have just taken the bull by the horns and gone for it. I like that in you. I look at how long I spent working for someone else, afraid to step out on faith and live my dreams. Then again, I did what I had to do to feed my three babies. I guess I couldn't really afford to quit my day job and follow a dream that could have potentially risked my children's well-being, Nope. That wouldn't have been fair to them, but I must say I'm very proud of you ladies. Now that I'm retired, I'll be looking for a business venture to invest in soon. I've always wanted to do something entrepreneurial wise. It'll come," I said.

"*Hmmmph.* Really? Well, we might just have an idea you'll be interested in," Maysa said.

I met with them for a few more business lunch dates and became so interested in what they presented that I shared the idea with my financial planner and lawyer, and voila, am now a silent business partner in an up-and-coming project. On the forefront, I mainly acted as the first point of contact for Diva's, greeting customers, scheduling appointments, and helping out in other areas where needed. What I found most appealing about being around these ladies was their positive energy, loyalty, and commitment to building one another up. Personally, as a fifty-plus-year-old woman, I welcomed being in the presence of their drive, vibe, and enthusiasm. I wholeheartedly supported women sharing what fuels other women to be empowered.

But most importantly, it was gratifying seeing the faces of women who after they came in for their fittings at the Isla's apparel shop, they were referred to Maysa who not only did their hair but also was a phenomenal make up artist. I saw firsthand the transformation of low spirits to high as women embraced themselves for the first time in their custom-made apparel and new faces professionally made up enhancing their natural beauty not the clown type that I see some ladies wearing at times such as the bat-like lashes, the heavily drawn on brows, and the caked on colored foundation especially some of the African-American women. Most ready-to-wear apparel off the racks of Macy's , Belk , Dillard's and similar retailers are not made for the unique body shapes we have, so for us to spend the money, time, and effort to get that individual style makes all the difference and does wonders for self-confidence. My mother always said if a woman looks good, she feels good.

But every now and then, one of us would need a little pick-me-up, and that's okay too. It was nice to be in a judge-free zone where we could vent about the plight of life, daily stress, and other small things. I was glad to have something different in my life to keep me active and productive.

Chapter Five

AS I WAS ABOUT TO get out the car, my phone vibrated, and it's my daughter India. Perfect timing, I thought as I answered the phone.

"Good morning," I sang into the phone.

"Hey Mom. How's it going? I miss you. You sound mighty chipper this morning. So...have you met any interesting men yet in your new hometown ?" India asked. Just like my wonderful daughter, cut to the chase.

"Nope, not yet. I'm in no hurry. I've been too busy focusing on getting me together first. I haven't had time to explore or even entertain the idea of meeting anyone new yet. Believe it or not, I'm just not ready. I'm way too busy for that. Anyhow, seems most of the guys I run into are either gay, already married, or in a relationship, and frankly, I'm not interested in any of those types," I responded.

"*Hmmmph.* I forgot you're one of those women who just doesn't need a man then. Is that right? 'Cause it's been almost two years or more since your last relationship, hasn't it?" India said India.

"Yes, it's been a few years but what's the rush and no, I'm not saying I don't need one, but what exactly do you want me to do, wear a sign that says I'm single and available? I'm not sure how I'm supposed to meet anyone at my age. I'm not going to hang out in bars or crap like that. Nope, I'm good. Besides, I've been too busy familiarizing myself with my new business partners."

Oh the angst of sharing all my personal experiences, India didn't know the depth and breath of my attachment to Fav, hardly anyone had known about our connection to one another. I kept that part of my life private. So for my daughter or anyone to think it had been a couple of years since I had had a relationship was simply not the case. But as far as I was concerned was none of their business. Yes, I considered it a connection to, not a relationship per se, in my mind there is a difference. Honestly, I wasn't sure if I had let go of Fav yet, was he the real reason I hadn't moved on, was it because there hadn't been any closure? I think about the closure piece on one hand then on another I still believe in God's will, if a thing is meant to be, it will be, if not let it go. As far as men and women relationships are concerned I am a bit old school, I still believe men are hunters and should pursue women and with that being said, I had conditioned myself accordingly, like I said before I knew I couldn't continue the same pattern with Fav, I wanted more but his actions showed me he didn't so I had to go. So back to the idea of closure, physically mission accomplished, mentally not so.

"Oh yeah, so how's that going? Oh, and by the way, I'm not suggesting you hang out in bars. That's hardly what I want to know whether my mom is hanging out in bars trying to pick up men. Just so you know, no one is just going to show up at your doorstep. But, *ummm,* yeah, back to your business, how are things working out?" India asked.

"Business is good actually, and just so you know, I'm a silent partner. I saw an opportunity that sounded good, so I invested, that's all. And two or three times a week, I help out where needed just to keep busy and to make a presence. You know, honey, I want you to also realize it's different for women my age now, especially when you have standards. You see, the dating scene is a lot different now. When I was younger, there seemed to be more social events where we had the opportunity to meet people, but things have changed so much, and I'm not into clubbing and meeting superfluous men. No, ma'am, Sam. Those days are over for me. I guess I'll be single a long time then," I answered.

"Okay. I get it. The bars are out. What about online dating? Have you considered that? It's time you got with the times now, Mom. We're in the twenty-first century. It might not be a bad idea for you to give it a try it, I'm just saying," India quipped.

"*Mmmm-hmm.* Sounds a little risky to me. Doesn't that mean I have to put all my personal information out on the internet? Sounds a little desperate to me," I said.

"*Ummm,* no. ffj ere's a way to do it. I'll FaceTime you later tonight. You get your laptop, and I'll walk you through it," India said.

"I don't know, child. Give me some time to research online dating first."

"Goodness, Mom. You're always so safe. Take a chance, girl. Try it. What harm can it do? If you don't get any hits from the site, you can always close your account. As a matter of fact, Miss Camille tried it, remember? That's how she met her husband."

"Yes, it was, wasn't it. *Mmmm,*" I responded.

Camille Hackett was a previous colleague of mine whom I had known for the past thirty years or so. We met when she was a divorcee with two children and I was living with Stetson , India's father. Because we were work buddies, we often shared life experiences, so she had experienced my relationship woes—the breakup with Stetson, and the marriage and divorce that involved Rad, Shea's father. She was also one of the few people at work who knew Stetson wasn't Zach's biological father and that I had been a teenage mother.

It had always amazed me Camille never really dated anyone back then, but that was back in the eighties. I knew she wasn't gay because she blatantly told us work friends one day during one of our girl chats. I had always admired how Camille sacrificed for her children, putting them first in everything she did. Well, come to find out, her son had been sexually molested by a family member during a babysitting scenario, so Camille had become overly protective of both of her children. It wasn't until the children were eighteen years old, maybe even older, and done with high school and had gone on to college that Camille finally decided to pursue dating again. Long story short, Camille had gone on a Christian dating site, and after a couple of duds as she had put it, she finally met the man of her dreams, married him, traveled the world and seemingly lived happily ever after. As it turned out, I was very happy for Camille, but I wasn't so sure those types of fairy tales happened for everyone.

"Okay, young lady, is that why you called, to discuss my love life? 'Cause if it was, let me assure you, don't worry about me. I promise I've made provisions for myself, so you, Zach, and Shea don't have to waste any sleepless nights fretting about taking care of me when I grow senile," I joked.

"Nope. That's not why I'm calling, Mother Dear. I wanted to hear your lovely voice and to let you know I ran into one of your old flames," India said.

"Oh God, say it isn't so. I'm afraid to ask. Who was that?" I responded.

Before answering, India snickered. "It was Deacon Xavier Fullerton. He asked how you were doing and said to tell you hello. He also wanted to know when you were coming back to Illinois. Of course I didn't hesitate to let him know you were never coming back, unless it's a death or some other emergency."

"Girl, I don't know what I'm going to do with you. I pop in occasionally to see y'all, but you know I don't want that old-ass man. He's so damn annoying. Everything you say to him, you have to repeat it. As I recall, our last conversation was before I left town. I saw him at Woodman's. I was like, 'Hey, Deacon Fullerton. How are you today?' Then he says, 'Happy Valentine's Day. Huh? What you talkin' about, Sister Twon?' Now mind you, it's January, so why on earth would I have said anything about Valentine's Day. So again, I repeated what I said but louder, hoping he heard me the second time around. Then I thought, Oh, brother, didn't nobody say anything about Valentine's Day. Where did he get that from? I just shook my head and kept it moving. Girl, I'm getting older, but I don't have the patience for that type of man. So, you don't have to tell Deacon Fullerton a thing about me, honey. I wish him well, and that's about it."

"Well, don't he wear a hearing aid? He don't look bad for an old guy. Just make sure he's got his hearing aid on, and you're all good," India teased.

"No, I've never seen him wear one. Although I heard him say he was prescribed one, but I guess he thinks he's too above wearing it, so he never uses it. I could tell that from one of our church meetings. It was so irritating having to always repeat stuff to him. Can you imagine how frustrating that would be living with someone like that? No, I'll pass. It's one thing if we were already married and I'd grown old with him and had to accept that, but since that's not the case, I'll pass."

India's laughter grew louder and louder from my dissertation about Deacon Fullerton. "I can't with you, Mom. I'm just saying there's options. Don't rule out a good prospect just 'cause of some age challenges. Some things have work-arounds."

"I got your work-arounds, girl. Work-arounds never worked well in my previous profession at the nuclear and electricity company. The only work-around I need to deal with is in my nightstand, now how you like that, Miss Smarty-pants."

I knew that would get her off the phone quick. The kids hated when I made even the slightest mention of my libido or the likes.

"*OOOO-weee*. TMI. *Yuk*. On that note, I gotta go, Mom. I'll call you later. Go have a glass of wine or something and relax. We'll talk after you've chilled a while. Oh, and another thing, Shea and I scheduled a flight to come see you for a long weekend in a couple of months. I'll text you our itinerary," India said.

"Okay honey. That's fine. I'm looking forward to it. I would love to have you guys here. I guess Zach can't get away, huh?" I said.

"I haven't talked to him lately, but we gave him a heads-up about our plans, and he didn't get back with us, so I take that as a no, he's not making this trip," India said.

"Alright, no problem. I'll reach out to him later. I know he's been putting in a lot of hours since he got that new promotion," I said.

Relocating hadn't only been good for me, but it seemed like it had been good for Zach, India, and Shea. All of them had to rely on themselves and were pretty successful at doing so. Sure, they had encountered life's difficulties and challenges, but for the most part, they had figured things out on their own without having to have me fix it for them. It had been a long time coming, but I was finally at a good place. I knew I had been a good mother and was still a good mother for my children.

Sure, I had gone through a period in my life when I blamed myself for much of their shortcomings, but in retrospect, I knew in my heart of hearts I raised those children right. They were raised in church with good morals and values. I taught them right from wrong, and whatever choices they made on their own, it was just that, their choices to make, and they had to deal with the consequences. Was it all good? No, it wasn't, and there were some very trying times I'll admit, but all in all, I gave them the best I had. Could I have done more? Perhaps, but it came a time where I couldn't continue to blame myself forever. And that time had come to an end for me. A good friend had said to me it was our maternal instinct to always want to help and support our children. I did that and more. It was my time now.

I was looking forward to spending time with India and Shea. We always had a good time laughing and talking together. The girls liked spending time with vacation mom. That was the name they jokingly gave me as we kidded around while together. So yes, it would be a welcome change when they came. I was thankful for our relationship.

TODAY WAS LIKE ANY OTHER typical day at the gym. It was around eight thirty-ish a.m. I used to go between six and seven-ish in the morning, but I changed that routine because I didn't want to run into Reverend Oliver Addison anymore. Truth be told, I didn't want to run into anyone who would interfere with my workout routine. The good reverend was just an acquaintance I recently met and definitely never made a pass at me or anything like that. It was just he liked to run his mouth too much, talking and what-not, and I just didn't feel like idle chitchatting in the morning. It was challenging enough mustering up the stamina to get to the gym, so when I got the notion to go, I wanted to make it worth my while, do what I was there for, and get done. Besides, working out was the therapy I needed to keep my mind off Fav and to move on with my life.

One thing I have learned is no matter what happens in life, you have to gather the strength and keep it moving, especially as it relates to relationships. I've had my heart broken to the point I thought I wouldn't recover, but in retrospect, rejection was actually protection. I wished I knew when I was sixteen and younger what I know now. I wouldn't have been in so damn a hurry to accept and settle for less than. It helps to love yourself first and to not be so desperate. Otherwise, you'll fall for the conniving schemes of any slick-talking man who comes your way.

So, here I am, nearing the end of my pace on the treadmill when out the corner of my eye, I notice a guy headed in my direction, although I pretended not to see him. But how could I not, with all he was wearing? Ray Charles could see him coming a mile away. He looked like he was in his late sixties or so. At first glance, it seemed by his demeanor he thought he was the shit. My rhythm was going so well on the treadmill and I was on the home stretch, so I refused to make any eye contact with anyone, particularly men. I was serious about my workout routine, so the last impression I wanted to give off was I was at the gym to pick up men.

"You know you would burn more calories by getting on that Life Cycle elliptical machine for fifteen to twenty minutes," said the guy, dressed in a red-and-white Nike workout apparel.

I maintained my stride on the treadmill and acted like I didn't hear his comment, but I was thinking, Did I ask for your help?

"Hey, I'm talking to you," Mr. Red Nike Apparel guy said.

I looked up with my best "Oh, are you talking to me?" look. But instead I said, "Oh, I'm sorry. Did you say something?"

"I said you would burn more calories by using the elliptical. I noticed you've been coming in here for the last few weeks doing the same routine. It may not be my business, but you look like a woman who's open to workout recommendations, seeing how you're so focused and all."

"Thank you. I might give it a try one day," I responded.

How rude, I thought. Did I ask for your help? Mental note never come to the gym at six a.m., too much traffic. Eight and nine-ish is out—don't want to run into talkative reverend. Maybe next, I'll try to come between one-thirty and two-ish. I used to do that, and it's much better, less traffic. There are no interruptions, and I don't have to make eye contact with anyone unless I want to.

Here was a case of my not wanting to be bothered. I always tried to be aware of my surroundings, especially as it related to guys walking up on me at the gym. I simply wasn't interested in getting to know men at the gym. I don't know why. It just wasn't my thing. Hell, maybe that was part of my problem, me trying to pick and choose where I met my next whomever. But judging from what I saw, it didn't appear a middle-aged guy in a red-and-white gym suit was my taste. I mean, I like fashion, but not to the point of overdoing it, and especially not while I'm trying to get my workout on. Not only did I find his style of dress overdone, this guy seemed overly confident to just approach me and offer advice when he didn't know me from a can of paint.

Where does he get off? I wondered. Keep it moving, playa. I'm not interested nor did I ask for your advice.

"Well, you should give it a try. I did, and I'm down thirty pounds just by doing fifteen minutes three to four days a week using that elliptical. It works, believe me. I won't kid you, you do have to build up to it. I started with just five-minute intervals. Now I can do thirty minutes or more at a time. Oh, and I apologize, my name is Clayton Carter."

"Nice to meet you. I'm Sabria Twon," I said as I extended my hand for a shake.

"The pleasure is all mine," Clayton said.

"So, don't let me keep you from your workout. I'm about to wrap things up here and head on out. I have a couple of errands to run, but I do appreciate the tip. I'll give it a try next time."

"No worries. You're not keeping me from anything, I've been here for a couple hours already. I was on my way out as well. I couldn't help but notice you again, so I decided to say something this time," Clayton said.

"Really, and may I ask, what do you mean by again and this time?" I asked apprehensively.

"Oh, I've seen you here several times before. I just hadn't taken the liberty to approach you, but since I didn't see a ring on your finger, I figured I'd stop by and say something to you."

"Well, I don't know about most people, but wearing jewelry of any kind is not typical for me when I'm working out, so because I'm not wearing a ring per se doesn't mean I don't have one."

"*Ummm-hmmm.* Yes, you're right. That's a good point. Are you married, seeing anyone, off the market?"

"Well damn, you're awful forward, aren't you? I just met you," I said.

"Hey look, I'm too old to play games. When I see someone I'm interested in, no need in wasting time. I'm too old for that. I apologize if I'm making you uncomfortable, but that's just how I see things. I think that's what's wrong with relationships today—too many games. Just say what you mean and do what you say. Life could be so much less complicated for all parties involved."

"Sounds interesting enough, and I agree with the not wanting to play games part," I said.

"Good. Well, at least we have that in common. Maybe next time we meet, you'll allow me to take you out for coffee, breakfast, or lunch. No pressure of course. Here's my card. Give me a call, and let me know when you're available. I would love to get together now, but I have an appointment I'm almost late for. It was my pleasure meeting you, and don't forget what I said about that elliptical machine. Try it and think about calling me," Clayton said.

"Likewise. The pleasure was all mine," I said.

I had to admit by now, Mr. Clayton Carter had piqued my interest to the point of me wanting to know more about him, along with the nerve and audacity to hand me a card and suggest I call him. I thought, *When hell freezes over.* Yes, I was somewhat interested but I come from the school of thought he should call me first. This dude had all the balls of a brass monkey, dressed in that red flashy getup. Who did he think he was or I was for that matter? It always amazed me the type of man I sometimes attracted. I realize dress wasn't everything. After all, materially speaking, that was something we could work on in the future, but for me, more important was his personality, integrity, and character. If those characteristics panned out, why not get to know him a little better?

Still, I wasn't too sure about his "Here's my card. Give me a call" approach either. That part seemed a bit extreme to me. I'm not that desperate. I would really have to give that one some thought. Hell, I wasn't looking for a husband, but it would be nice to go out with a male companion occasionally for conversation, dinner, a movie, or whatever for a change of pace. *Hmmmph.* So, that was when I mentally decided to let my guard down and go with the flow to see how this meet-and-greet played out.

Chapter Six

IT HAD BEEN QUITE SOME time—in fact, it had been practically a year and a half, not that I   had kept track—since I last saw Fav, and I was trying to give it my all in moving forward. I didn't know what my future held in terms of romance, but I was bound and determined I wasn't going back to the past. The one thing I knew for sure was I needed to move on, especially since I hadn't so much as received a text let alone a call from Fav.

As I got in my car, I was reminded of a conversation I had with my friend Suni. She said when you're single and over fifty, everything comes to a screeching halt. Suni had tried several online dating sites and wasn't afraid to play her hand meeting prospective dates via the internet. My thoughts were interrupted by my phone.

"Hey, girl. You must have been reading my mind. I was just thinking about your crazy behind. What's up?"

"Hey. I figured I'd catch you in your car. Are you leaving the gym now?" Suni asked.

"Yes, ma'am. I sure am, and you'll never guess what happened today," I said.

"What, girl? Did you meet a man?" Suni asked.

"Well damn, Suni. As a matter of fact, yes, I did."

"Well, what does he look like, girl? I hope he has a body since you met his ass at the gym."

"Now, you know that don't mean a thing. There are so many perpetrators at that place, women and men."

"Yeah, you got that right."

"He didn't look that bad though once I actually decided to look at him."

I shared the events of my meeting play-by-play with my friend since I know Suni is a detailed-oriented person. She always had a listening ear, especially as it related to stories about women dating new men, ideas to find men, or any topic of the like.

"Actually, I thought about you 'cause when I saw what he was wearing, I was totally not interested. Then after talking with him for a little bit, I heard your voice in my head saying, 'You can't always judge a book by its cover,' so that made me loosen up a bit. Surprisingly, I began to find him a bit intriguing, and for an old guy, he didn't look that bad. He had nice teeth and was clean shaven. He even had the smooth salt-and-pepper thang going on, so you know, I was sort of letting my guard down a little. Although I still think he was a bit bold to come at me the way he did. But what the hell? I guess when you're that age, you figure you don't have much time left to beat around the bush."

"Girl, you're crazy, but good point," Suni said.

We both laughed.

"So, what's next? Did you give him your number?" Suni asked.

"See, that's the part I'm stuck at. He handed me a card and asked me to give him a call. Really...who does that? Is that what we're on in today's society in America? I mean, I'm not used to having to be the initiator, seems to me if he was that interested, he would call me. Do I appear that hungry for a date? Dude got me doing a self-evaluation, and I don't even know him like that."

"Girl, some of these men are so trifling these days, but you know my dumb ass would wait a couple days and call that man   just so I could hear what he had to offer. We're living in different times now, Bria. Its's okay for women to approach men, so go ahead and call him. He got me curious," Suni said.

"Honey, I'm just not comfortable with it yet. I'll admit my interest is somewhat piqued, but my inner gut tells me there's something there I can't put my finger on, so I'm hesitant. I'm not opposed to talking with him again if or when I see him at the gym, but as far as calling him first, well, I'm not quite there yet. Call me old-fashioned or whatever. I still believe in the adage 'men are hunters.' If they want you, they come for you."

"That's where you and I differ, girlfriend. See, you've been married once—basically twice if you count the common law relationship with Stetson. You've always been in long-term relationships until the last what two or three years, so what I'm trying to tell you is the game has changed. I don't wait. Hell, if I did, I would be dried up and shriveled out," Suni said.

"Suni, what am I going to do with you? You're crazy as hell."

"Naw. I'm just keeping it one hundred, period. Do you know how long I've been single? I'm still trying to find my husband, and I'm sixty-four. Why do you think I join so many dating sites? I don't have time to wait, that's why."

"Funny you mentioned the dating sites. Just the other day, India and I had a conversation about me joining one. You know times must be hard when you have to resort to taking advice from your daughter to assist you with joining a dating site to meet men. *Ummm,* I'm still not sold on that idea yet," I said.

"Girl, get you a bottle of that wine you like. What's it called again?" Suni asked.

"Voga Italia Pinot Grigio." I said.

"Yeah, that'll get your courage up. Go for it, and let me know when you do. Anyhow, I just called to check in with you today. I'm at my doctor's appointment, so I'll get back with you later." Suni responded.

"Okay. See if that doctor can get your mind right while you're in there." I said.

"Girl, if he wasn't married, I'd be trying to let him get something else right," Suni said, laughing.

"Bye, girl. I can't with you. I'll call you tomorrow." I said.

"Cool. Bye." Replied Suni.

Whew I knew Suni could be too much at times. But I still loved her though. She's the true essence of resiliency, I always used to tease her she has nine lives because she beat cancer twice—once with ovarian cancer, then with breast cancer—not to mention the knee and eye surgeries she'd had. During each ordeal, she handled each event with amazing strength and courage like I had never seen. One thing about Suni was she always relied on her faith in God and her humor to carry her through. I guess those were the attributes I admired about her the most. She never let anything get her down. She just kept it moving— when life dealt her lemons, she made lemonade.

Over the years, my circle of friends had dwindled and wasn't large, but what I did have was a strong network and support group of girlfriends I could rely on when the going got tough. In life, I've learned to prioritize what's important. No man is an island, that was a phrase my mother used to remark so often. I never knew what it meant until I got older, but it rings so true. Everyone needs a good support group. Good thing I had sense enough to know I needed one throughout my lifetime. What I will say is this: A few good sister-friends should consist of women you can trust, confide in, and on occasion drank (yes drank not drink) with without being judged. Yes, every woman needs the strength of another woman.

Most importantly, I'd learned how to be a good friend and how to cultivate relationships. I'd become better at reaching out to the people who meant the most to me. Sometimes, a quick call or text was all it took just to say, "Hey, how you doing?" to let a person know how much they were thought of. I've come to realize, with so much going on in our society today, personal and political, we need an out to relieve the stress. Afterall, it was my sisterhood with my girlfriends that got me through the most critical moments in my life. Otherwise, I might not have been able to cope.

I looked at my dash and saw the time, 10:23. I had better run by the car wash before heading home, I had enough time to go to Walgreen's to have my eye drop prescription filled, by then it should be closer to eleven. I justified eating an early lunch , I made a mental note to stop by Paradise Café and grab a grilled chicken fuji salad. Oh, how those gave me life. Today's workout was exhausting, not to mention my mind was racing wondering whether to call Mr. Carter.

"Helllll naw," I said out loud.

Life for me had been pretty amazing since I had retired from the nuclear electric plant three years ago. I found myself at a peaceful place because I had finally learned to do what I wanted to do first. My children were all grown now   and successful in their own rights. Zora, India's daughter, had grown up and was off to college . For so many years, I basically put the needs of my family first, delaying what I wanted to do since I had always been the provider. Even when I was married, I felt an obligation to be there for my children. Sure, life wasn't perfect, but for the most part, I was happy. Depending on how I felt, my time was divided between walking, working out at Planet Fitness, and occasionally helping the girls over at Diva's. I wasn't one of those people who had a set routine. I just knew I had to have some sort of movement in my life. I wish I could say I was like all those other fitness guru types who stuck to their exercise plan, but that just wasn't me. I had thought about volunteering with my new church with one of those grow groups,   which happened to be another name for ministry. I liked the idea because the church offered a variety of groups, such as for singles, divorcées, married couples, and so on, but I was cautious about getting myself too tied up in activities as I had done for so many years back home. Sounded simple. It was, and that was fine with me. No hustle or bustle, just the simplicity of life. The less drama, the better.

Sometimes I couldn't believe how much time I spent trying to please other people and how I had tried to be everything to everybody but me. I had finally learned to stop and had to literally say to myself, "Hey, you. What about me, Bria Twon?"

If I had the chance, I would tell my younger self not to be so hard on myself. You can have anything to which you set your mind on as long as you remain focused; and of course, put in the work.   That's what I would say to my younger self.

For me, I do a lot of reflecting because I can't forget that little girl who grew up believing she wasn't good enough or that I didn't matter, and even when given affirmations that I received from others outside the home I grew up in, I still lacked confidence. I tried to dim my light and veer to the background because I didn't want to stick out as the girl who thought she was better than anyone else, especially when she came from such a tainted background. It had taken all these years for me to realize I am somebody, and I'm here because I deserve to be. It doesn't matter how I got here, but I am here and damnit. I'm going to make the best of my time in the present as I can. I haven't always made the best decisions to change how I approached and handled some aspects along my journey as it related to my personal growth.

My spirit, body, and mind depended on these changes if I were to live a life full of joy, peace, and happiness. For my spiritual being, I learned to meditate every day, first thing in the morning before my feet touched the floor. The mornings are the quietest. It's in the still of the morning when I'm alone with myself and my thoughts that I'm listening to my inner gut intuition—that voice from God speaking to me, directing my path and telling me how to proceed. You have to be able to enjoy being with yourself away from the noise of life and influences of others. I found for me, that's when I'm the most creative, I can think more clearly, and most importantly, I'm at peace. There's truth in the scripture. Be still and know.

Seems the older I get, I'm more interested in a fit body, so I have to constantly force myself to maintain my fitness routine. When I don't make it to the gym, I try to at least walk four miles. Sometimes I even turn on my playlist and dance around my room—something, anything to get some movement. Some days, I'm at the gym thirty minutes to an hour; other days longer, depending on how I feel. The key is I'm not in competition with anyone. I'm doing it for me and my well-being, so there's no judgment however long or short I decide to stay. The point is I'm doing it. I've learned not only does working out help me lose weight, but it gives me such profound clarity as it pertains to whatever life decisions I have to make.

Protecting my mind is one of the biggest improvements I've decided to make in my life. One of the first things I decided to do was get rid of the negative energy around me. It didn't matter where it came from—family, friends, colleagues, relationships—they had to go. I decided I couldn't become a better person and keep negativity around me. All it does is suck the life out of you. I was tired of having people suck the life out of me. For too long, I had been a people pleaser, although I had been one with leadership tendencies, if that makes sense.

On a personal level, girlfriends always reached out to me for advice, but why? Was it because I was so ingenious, and if so, then why was my life so jacked up? Or perhaps it was that I had become so clever at masking my shortcomings and giving off the impression I had it all together because I had had the six-figure salary job, had bought two houses, been married twice, bought finer cars, and wore designer clothes and shoes that managing the lives of others made me the most likely candidate of my circle when in fact what I was really doing or had done was neglected my own space, so that's where I fell short.

Whatever the case, I looked up literally, and now I'm about to be sixty years old, and I wondered where the years had gone when it suddenly dawned on me I might not have much time left, so I had better fend for myself and let others around me figure it out for themselves. Which brings me to my point about relationships and the importance of my choice to cultivate one. My life is mine. I value it, so every second, minute, hour, day, I want as much positive energy as possible in my flow of life.

I no longer tried to manage other people's lives, particularly my grown children, family, and friends, and by the same token, I refused to be bothered by their manipulative influences toward me. When I feel a negative vibe from someone, I separate myself from the situation. Over the course of my life's journey, I had been in enough unhealthy relationships for me to know I'm done practicing bad behaviors or being subjected to them. Einstein's law of insanity is real. Doing the same thing over and over and expecting a different result is insanity. I knew in order for new things, people, places to manifest in my life, I had to start with me, so I decided to get motivated and set specific goals about what I wanted in every aspect of my life, which is one reason I was single by choice. I was done thinking something was wrong with me, that I was unlovable, or I wasn't getting chosen because no one wanted me. No, I was on a journey of self-discovery, evolvement, growth, and development.

But every now and then, I gave in to my female human erotica, meaning I thought about sex and good sex with a man, not just any man, with Fav. Oh, how I longed for his touch again. He was one of my biggest weaknesses, and I knew it. I wasn't strong enough to leave him alone nor had I ever made my feelings known to him. I couldn't pinpoint my reasoning for this. Was it because I didn't know my worth? Was I afraid that had I let him know how I felt he would leave me alone for good? Maybe. All I knew was I was like a dog waiting on a bone.

He texted, "hey, you," and I took off like a leapfrog. It didn't matter how intermittent the texts would be—once a month, every two months, the time. I had chosen to fulfill my needs with Fav. I was so lost. I had to leave because I didn't have any clarity, and I knew the longer I stayed, I became more and more engulfed in unhappiness with myself. At one point, I thought I loved him, then at another I thought how can I love someone who hasn't shown any sign he loved me. It was like I had this secret life—hell, no one even knew all of what I was going through . Me, the secret keeper, I was so good at it. I guess that's the trait of being an enabler for the majority of my life.

I believed in timing, which was everything to me, so with that said, in time perhaps, I would find more or maybe even want more. For now, I was just enjoying the ride. I just needed to rediscover me and know my worth. I needed a clear heart. I needed to know what I wanted, no sex involved, a clean slate. Then once I figured that out, I would have to put me first. I may not be perfect, but I'm worth it.

Chapter Seven

SO BACK TO MY REALITY. I was at Diva's where I enjoyed being around the trendy fashion, upbeat music, and decor. Fashion fuels my inner creativity and outward personality. I'd always felt my best self when I dressed. Clothes and fashion were my way of empowerment. I considered myself a trendsetter and not a follower, so it was fun being around like-minded women who didn't follow the rules as it related to what was in and what wasn't, but rather what complemented and was most flattering to the individual woman. As usual, clients came in and left with a renewed sense of belonging, confidence, and pride.

I don't know who it was therapeutic for the most, me, the customers, or the owners. At the end of the day, we all got something out of it. Seems we knew where to destress, which was why we kept going back to Diva's. We were magnetically drawn to the support we got from one another there. Our individual lives craved it as much as the air we breathed. Inspiration flowed from heart to heart from a wide age spectrum. It didn't matter whether it was a thirty-year-old or eighty-year-old lady. Oh yeah, occasionally someone brought in one of the elders for a makeover, and some of those ladies were just as feisty as a woman in her fifties. I enjoyed hearing the tales from women who had experienced similar situations as me like a cheating or substance-addicted husband. Just hearing how they handled these scenarios gave other women like me wisdom. It was also encouraging for a middle-aged woman going through midlife crisis or sometimes even a younger one who for whatever reason seemed invincible who when she is at that stage and thinks she knows everything to get an older women's perspective. It's not to say the younger ones always listened, but at least they got good food for thought. The point is, you didn't leave there the same way you came. There was always someone willing to be transparent enough to share their story, which encouraged all of us to look inside ourselves and find a new place. We found the courage to move on. That's just how it was at the spot. No mess, no drama, and no fuss.

"How ya doing today, Ms. Bria?" Maysa asked.

"Hey, girl. I'm great. How are you today? And how was that date last night? That's what I want to hear about," I said.

"*Awww*, girl, wasn't nothing jumping. He thought it was going to be, but I stuck to my guns. It wasn't. I told y'all, I'm done with his foolishness. He has talked reckless to me for the last time, and I'm tired of it. He always calls back as if nothing has ever happened. Well guess what, I'm sick of it. He can kick rocks," Maysa said.

"Well, okaaay. So how are you feeling about all this? Did you two at least get a chance to talk about where you are in the relationship? I know you said there were some things you wanted to get off your chest and all, so did you get any answers?" I asked.

"Girl, bye with him. It's either his way or the highway, and you know what, I'm not having it. So basically, all we did was end up fighting, and as usual, nothing got resolved. Absolutely nothing," Maysa said.

"Well, honey, I don't know why you keep putting yourself through that. All I can say is when you get tired, you'll know," I said.

"Ms. Bria, I know. I just wish I could be more like you. You don't let nothing bother you," Maysa said.

"*Hmmmph.* Now, I wouldn't go that far. There are aspects in relationships that do bother me. I guess that's why I'm not in one, remember? I've been in enough to know when to go on pause and take a time-out, and right not, I've made a conscience choice to put me in time-out if you know what I mean," I said.

"Yeah, girl. I feel you," Maysa said.

"Well, don't stress about it too much, sweetie. You're a beautiful woman, full of potential, with a hell of a lot to offer. The right one will come along soon, you just wait and see. You don't have to accept anyone's sloppy seconds. You just remember that, honey. Don't be in such a rush," I said.

"Thank you, Ms. Bria, I just love you," Maysa said.

"I love you too. Now go on and have a great day. We'll talk later."

Out of all the three ladies, I was drawn to Maysa the most. She was warm, kindhearted, and full of humor and spirit. The other two ladies were married with families and seemed to have great relationships and everything going for themselves. Maysa, on the other hand, had been seeing this guy for the last three years or so, and in all of our opinion, he wasn't worthy of the weight of a grain of sand. I personally believed she overcompensated with humor to mask hurt and pain, but who was I to judge? From our personal one-on-ones, she had confided in me some of the issues between her and the so-called significant other in her life. There were times I literally wanted to slap the stuff right out of his fat black ass. But because she was my friend, I didn't place judgment on her situation. I merely listened and offered an opinion when and only when she insisted. Over the years, I had learned that was best when dealing with my girlfriends' issues with their significant others. We've all had issues with men, and sometimes we just needed a listening ear. Most times, we know what's best for us. We don't want someone telling us what they would do and wouldn't put up with and all the other blah, blah, blah. Sometimes we just wanted to vent. But even then, there were times when I blew a fuse, as I tended to do sometimes, out of love and care for my friend. I knew it was one of my downfalls though. That whole idea of withholding my inner thoughts or being too opinionated about another individual's situation was a bit mind boggling for me, especially as it related to redundant stories of unworthy partners. Because of all I had gone through in my past relationships, some shit was just not tolerable to me. So, after time after time of hearing yet another bad experience of how Maysa's so-called boo had treated her, I would resort to fits of what the hell is wrong with you and fuck him type of conversation, which I would later regret because deep down I knew she wasn't ready to change her situation. The last thing I wanted to do was add to my friend's pain, but I certainly didn't want her to be blindsided either. I can't count on one hand how many times we had scenarios such as those where I would later have to apologize for my tone and what I said because I felt like I was being too harsh. But was I? She was my girl. Shouldn't I be able to go hard with her to help her, no matter how abrupt I seemed? Especially since I knew I had her back?

Nevertheless, I would end up apologizing because I was trying to work on myself, and one of the things I was trying to clean up was the dirty mouth stuff. I still had a long way to go though. The one thing I liked about Maysa though was she didn't seem to mind when I had these keep-it-real convos with her. In fact, I would say to her, "Do you want the raw, uncut version of my opinion or the new censored version?" And she would say, "Naw, girl, give me the old raw uncut 'cause that's the one I can relate to." Even so, I would be remorseful for how I conveyed the message to my friend even though she had given me the green light.

I guess I struggled so much with it because this was something I used to do in my previous relationships, rather than discuss an important matter at the onset, I would let it fester and build up then I would erupt with emotion. I knew emotional repression was a weakness for me, so was profanity when I got emotional, which was why I vowed to get better. Oh, I could've used the excuse that I had had it up to my neck in hearing about what he did and said to her that was highly uncalled for or that I was provoked by his egregious behavior toward her, but that wasn't the point. The point was no matter what I said to her about him, it wasn't going to make her act any sooner than when she was ready to change her situation. Maysa's case reminded me of something I heard one of her clients say. She said she knew it was time to part ways from her husband because she was tired of being sick and tired.

I knew only too well that sometimes when we ladies make up our minds to be with a man, we ignore all the signs, even though the red flags are blatant. Hell, a two-year-old could see some of the stuff we chose to ignore, but that's just how we do, then we try to justify the right-in-our-face stuff when we want or think we have to have and need certain individuals in our lives. So, the last thing my friend needed to hear was someone telling her, "Girl, I wouldn't take that." When most of us don't know what we would take or do if we were in those shoes. All I knew was I was going to be there for my girl—whatever she needed, I would be there. Meanwhile, I kept encouraging her, reminding her she's worth more than being with someone who is so disrespectful and inconsiderate of her feelings, in the hopes one day she'd get it.

We got through the close of another day at the shop with clients coming and going and each lady doing her own thing with her business as usual. Out of nowhere, we hear a loud commotion coming from the back of the building.

"What the hell was that?" Maysa yelled, coming from the upstairs salon.

"I don't know. Sounds like something's going on outside. Better look out and see what's going on, Girl, you are not going to believe this, but look across the street out back. Is that a car on the railroad tracks?" I replied.

"A car? Are you serious? Let me see," Maysa said as she focused on the view. "Well, damnit that girl better be able to explain this, that's my niece Olivia's car, how the hell did she get it on that track like that?" Maysa asked.

By now, both of us had surrounded the window to peer out toward the noise in the distance. What we saw was incredible. A gold-tone Dodge Neon sat too low on the ground to be a train caboose had its four tires perpendicular to the railroad tracks as if it was a train ready to roll. The only problem was, it was a car on the tracks, and it was stuck. The question was how did it get there.

The silence was broken by a pounding on the front door of the building. Instantly, I thought, it's a good thing Diva's main doors were locked and they had a security system. With so much going on in the world, it was safer that way. Typically, the receptionist would check the surveillance monitor before allowing anyone in, but apparently she was away from her station. I watched as Maysa ran to look at her control panel, which was mounted on the wall. It also included a screen so she could see who was at the door. I saw her expression change.

"Olivia, what the hell is going on?" Maysa yelled.

After seeing the car, it occurred to me it belonged to Maysa's niece. Olivia was a sixteen-year-old who not long ago had gotten her driver's license. During some of our previous girl chats, Maysa had shared with me she was Olivia's legal guardian. Olivia was the child of Maysa's brother who was on crack. So was her mother. Maysa got her when she was an infant and had raised her like her own. Maysa admitted to overcompensating due to the absence of Olivia's biological   parents. Olivia was spoiled and seemed to find pleasure in drama or trouble of some sort, and Maysa was habitually bailing her out. But this time, we didn't know how she was going to explain getting that car on the railroad tracks or how they would get it off.

Olivia was bawling, saying she was sorry. She meant to turn down the street and something about being distracted, and before she knew it she was on the railroad tracks. She thought it was the street, she didn't realize it was tracks, and so on and so forth. I just shook my head and got my things so I could go on home. Another thing I had learned was how to mind my own business. Unless it was life or death, some things just didn't warrant my getting involved. I said good night to the Maysa, I patted her on the back and whispered in her ear a comforting, "It's going to be alright," reminded her to reset her alarm, be safe and said I'd see her tomorrow, then I left. I was sure I would find out later what really happened.

Chapter Eight

I THOUGHT I WOULD GET an earlier start at the gym after the day I'd had yesterday, so I decided to get there by 6:30 a.m. Besides that, I figured it would give me time to do my thirty- to forty-five-minute workout and get out before the other retirees got there, meaning the crowd in general but the men in particular. Especially Mr. Red Nike Apparel guy with the Mercedes ring. Oh yeah, as I recollected from our first acquaintance, how could I not notice that gaudy diamond Mercedes emblem on his right index finger? Anyhow, I still wasn't up to any idle chitchat and specifically not any with him.

"So, you just want to keep me hanging, huh? I thought I would have heard from you by now. So, what, you trying to avoid me? I thought your regime was between eight thirty nine in the morning. Looks like you might have gotten here earlier. What brings you out so early this morning?" Clayton asked.

Damn, I think, but I say, "Well good morning to you." Without any regard to what I heard spoken, I finished my last second or two of my cool down on the treadmill. I completed my session, got my iPhone and water, used the towel I had around my neck to wipe the perspiration from my face then turned, and there stood Clayton. I looked him right in his eyes to let him know I had no reason to explain nor did I owe him any explanation as to what time I did my workout.

"Yes, good morning, and indeed it is a great morning. How about you join me for brunch? Are you available? Has anyone ever told you how naturally beautiful you are? I'm sorry I don't mean to sound so fresh, but it's true, and like I told you when we first met, when I see someone I like, I don't waste time. I'm too old for that. I would imagine you are too. What are you about fifty-three, fifty-four..."

"Uh, excuse me, but you're rather personal and quite a bit forward, don't you think?" I replied.

"My apologies. I didn't mean any harm. Quite the contrary. I absolutely meant it as a compliment. Come on, we're two grown people. Don't you know how to accept a compliment from a man? Your skin is flawless, your eyes are mesmerizing, and your scent is captivating. I'm so drawn to you. It had to be divine order for us to meet here this morning. So, how about it? Don't turn me down. Let's meet for brunch, lunch—your call. Just say when, where, what time. I won't take no for an answer. Come on, beautiful lady. How about it? I'm just trying to get to know you a little better, that's all. Baby steps. So, what do you say?" Clayton said, extending his hand to lead me from the treadmill.

I stood there frozen, not knowing what to make of all he had said. My mind was going a hundred miles per hour. Is he for real? What kind of shit is this? Is this guy a psychopath? Then, I heard my friend Suni's voice in my head saying, "Girl, you need to let down your guard some. Your expectations are too high." It was at that moment when I decided to say fuck it. I had to ask myself, How are you ever going to meet anyone if you keep comparing them to Fav ? Why not meet the guy for chat? I could do so in a public place and drive my own vehicle—no harm, no foul.

After all, I wasn't looking for a husband, just a little male companionship. I didn't see anything wrong with that. Was Clayton a bit overconfident? I thought, yes, but why not see what he was really like underneath that bold exterior? I seem to always welcome a challenge. Again, I had to be honest with myself. Clayton's direct approach certainly had gotten my attention, which made me curious enough to want to know more about him.

"Okay, Mr. Won't Take No for an Answer. At least let me check my schedule. I'm not saying yes, but a strong possible. I still have your number. I'll give you a call to let you know what works for me. How's that?" I reached for my towel and grabbed my phone to leave. "You know what on second thought, why don't I call you right now that way you have my number. I have your card right here in my phone case, let me press in these digits, let's see if the service works in here, it should, looks like it ringing, there you go, answer your phone. Walla, we're done.

Now you have my number, save it to your contacts. You know how to do that right?" I said sarcastically.

"You got jokes this morning I see. 815...where's that?" Clayton asked.

"That's an Illinois area code. Give me a couple days and we'll go from there." I said as I preceded to leave.

"Hey, if that's how it has to be, then that's the way it is. I'll be waiting with expectancy for the days to pass. I'll call you in a few days, that should give you more than enough time to check your schedule busy lady," Clayton said.

Chapter Nine

WHAT A WAY TO START my day. I hope this isn't any indication of how the rest of the day is going to go. Well, at least I got my workout out of the way so now I can focus on other things. Just as I was about to walk out to the parking lot, I looked down at my phone to see I had three missed calls from Maysa. Wow, I wonder what's going on. I tapped her name to give her a call back.

"Hey, girl. What's wrong. Is everything alright?"

Immediately I could tell by her voice she'd been crying.

"No, it's not. Where are you? Can you meet me at the salon like right now? Oh my God, I'm about to lose it. I swear I am.

Please, Ms. Bria. I need you to come right now before I do something to somebody I'm sure I'll regret," Maysa said.

"Sure. I'm just leaving the gym. I should be there in about twenty minutes. I'm on my way. You try to calm down. I don't want you getting your blood pressure up or anything like that."

I had to go and check on my friend Maysa. Although she was in her early forties and me in my late fifties, she reminded me a lot of myself when I was her age. By nature, Maysa was an old soul. She was wise and always saw the good in most everyone she met. So, for her to call sounding as if her world was about to shatter meant something terrible had to have happened. Through previous girl chats, Maysa and I had shared some in-depth details about men and relationship issues, so I immediately thought the crisis had to do with her male friend.

When I arrived, I didn't bother parking in the designated employee space at the back of the building. Instead, I pulled up in front right near the door so I could walk straight in. Unknown to me at the time, Maysa must have been thinking the same way as me because her Range Rover was parked in front as well. Suddenly, I became panicked as I pulled my vehicle to the tailgate of her SUV and pushed my ignition to shut off my car. I had barely reached the entrance when Maysa swung open the storefront door.

"Girl, I got here as fast as I could. Is anyone sick, dead, or near death. What's going on?" I anxiously asked, trying to remain composed.

"You won't believe what that bastard did. I swear, I could kill him. I'm so sorry to get you in this, but I had to have someone to talk to who I knew I could trust. And no, nobody's sick, dead, or near death. I should have said that upfront. But hell, it's almost just as bad."

"Okay, so now you're scaring me. What is it?" I probed.

"Okay, Ms. Bria. Let's go upstairs to the salon so we can talk in private," Maysa said.

"Come on, girl. Shiiid, you got my nerves worked up. I sure hope you got something to drink up there."

I could barely remember if I had turned my ignition off. I was feeling so discombobulated and concerned when it occurred to me in my vehicle I had the convenience of the push and hold engine start button on the center console. Since time was of the essence, thank God for that feature. All I knew was I just got out the car, and hopefully, I had remembered to touch the doors to lock it up. At this point, I was just trying to get to my friend as fast as I could to hear what was going on. Sometimes Maysa could be a little over the top and overdramatized things to the hundredth power, but still, she was my girl, and I had her back, no matter what was going on.

"Girl, let me tell you what Olivia said is the reason why she was so upset last night and mistakenly drove that car onto the railroad track. First of all she said she had been over to Stephanie's house for a little get-together for Steph's birthday. I guess she had a few of her friends and their fellas were there as well. Second, come to find out the punch she had been drinking at Stephanie's had apparently been spiked. Olivia was clearly inebriated, I could tell by her behavior, her speech was slurred and her balance was off, she definitely was not her normal self." Explained Maysa.

"What! Oh my goodness, she's a minor, that could have gone way bad on so many levels." I said.

"Exactly and don't think I didn't give Stephanie's ass the business about her having those teens over there wilding out. I mean I know teens will try to get away with stuff but not on my watch, there is just too much going on today. These teens don't need any further bulls eye on their backs as it relates to trouble and being stopped by the police. See, Olivia knows she can't pull that nonsense with me. Silly me for letting my guard down and allowing her to go by Stephanie's as often as I did anyhow. Olivia said she always stopped over there because Steph's man had been sort of acting as a father figure to her—acting like he had her best interest, guiding her on the maintenance of her car and stuff like that. You know, Olivia really had trust in him. So neither me or Olivia didn't think anything of it either, of course. I always had my eye on him 'cause you know I don't trust too many men who cater to young girls, and I don't care who they are."

"Okay. So, who's Stephanie, honey? Help me out. I'm trying to keep up. It's a good thing that railroad track is no longer used, that would have been horrific had a train came along while that child was driving on that track," I said.

"Girl, you met my cousin Stephanie a few months ago at the shop. Remember? She was the one who was getting the long red weave put in her hair, talking about she and her man were celebrating their twentieth anniversary, and they ain't even married, and she wanted to add some fire to spice things up. That's why she wanted that long-ass red hair. Now you remember?"

"Oh, okay. Yeah, I do, so go on," I said as I poured a glass of pinot grigio into the wineglass Maysa set on the counter.

"Yeah well, you haven't heard the best of it yet. Get this, how about Stephanie's so-called man or whatever he is been eyeing Olivia all the time? Olivia said when she and her bestie left Stephanie's little pre-celebratory gathering that night, she stopped by the QT for gas. How about that sleaze bag pulled up and approached Olivia at the gas station out of nowhere? He said he liked her outfit and she looked nice, then he offered to fill her tank up supposedly out of kindness. Olivia said he claimed it was his way of helping her out because he had noticed how focused and smart she was. He said he wanted to help her succeed." Said Maysa.

"Help her succeed? What does your cousin Stephanie think about him wanting to help Olivia? Sounds like some frackle nackle bullshit to me," I stated.

"You think I don't know, that's exactly what it is. Ms. Bri, he was propositioning her. Hell, Olivia said the punk even offered to upgrade her car and get her a new one, all she has to do is be nice to him—that it would be their little secret. Olivia said it shook her to the core, but she was scared because it was late and she was alone, so she tried to play along with him. She said she told him thanks, that was nice of him, but she was okay and would manage without his help. Then the bastard says, 'Well take my number and call me if you ever need anything,' then he throws her a twenty-dollar bill like she's some desperate chick. Girl, the nerve of that muthafucka. Olivia is so outdone. She really trusted him. He would give those young girls play-by-play rules on how men try to use women, and here all along, he's one of the very men he tried to school her on," Maysa said.

"First of all why in the world does she have so many responsibilities and she is sixteen? Her focus should be school, getting good grades, and preparing for college. Oh my God. Yeah, that's lowdown, that's for sure. Goes to show he was up to no good. How is it he leaves a gathering done on his and Stephanie's behalf? So, what are you going to do? Are you planning on telling Stephanie? 'Cause I can assure you if she's been with him for twenty-something years, this isn't the first time he's pulled this sort of thing, and you can best believe she knows the kind of man he is. She won't believe you. She'll say you're jealous of her relationship and so forth. She might even go as far as to say Olivia is lying. I would just let that bastard know you know about it, so he knows he got the wrong one this time. That's a damn shame. I wonder how many young girls he has out on a limb like that already. How pathetic?"

"See that was part of our agreement, I supply her basic needs anything over and above she has to work and buy herself, and she was supposed to be saving for college as well. Her situation is complicated. She's been through a lot and I help her as best I can. Still I don't care. I want to tell Stephanie to tell her freakin' man to lay off my niece. His ass needs to get busted," Maysa said.

"Okay. So, let me ask you this: How much do you value your relationship with Stephanie?"

"I love her. She's my cousin, but we're not that damn close. I have closer bonds with girlfriends than I do with her."

"Well, I'm asking for a reason, Maysa. She's been with him for twenty-plus years. He's never married her, so do you think she cares what you tell her about the love of her life? She doesn't. Go ahead, tell her, but let him know for sure that if he so much as comes near Olivia, he'll be sorry he did. Olivia is who I care about, and as her caregiver, you should protect her and hopefully any other young girl who he could potentially victimize, but Stephanie, she's a lost cause. It's sad to say, but there are some women who sell their souls just to have any old piece of a sorry-ass man. Unfortunately, Stephanie is one of the leaders of the pack."

"Yeah, she is. Olivia said she thought it was weird he was always liking her Facebook pictures and shit all the time too. Whew, every time I think about that punk, I get pissed. Dirty bastard," Maysa said.

"I could never understand how some women allow their husbands or significant others to do that anyhow. Seems creepy to me, and what the hell is he doing being Facebook friends with a sixteen-year-old female anyhow? That's just wrong on so many levels. See, like I said, you think Stephanie doesn't already know what she got. She does. She just doesn't want to admit it, fear of being alone, she's in denial, all of that. Oh well, I pity the fool. That shit is wrong."

"You pity who, Stephanie or him?"

"Definitely not him. I feel sorry for Stephanie because somewhere down the road, she lost her self-value. Hell, I don't know if she ever had any. It begs to wonder what she's really been through for her to accept a man who doesn't respect their relationship. I guess what I'm saying, Maysa, is things aren't always what they seem. It goes deeper than what you or I know. That's why I try not to be so judgmental. I know what it's like to lose yourself in a man—in others period. Until you get to a point of truth within yourself, you'll always accept less than. But right now, the immediate issue is Olivia and protecting her. I'm glad she didn't fall for his stuff," I said.

"You have to let Olivia know she can trust you to be there for her. First of all, let her know it wasn't her fault his trifling ass approached her, then let her know what to do to keep herself safe from any future scenarios like that. What I know about these instances is a man like that sees a young girl like Olivia whose mother is in and out of her life, so he figures Olivia is desperate for anything, especially easy money as well as material things," I said.

"It's similar to boys and girls who fall prey to gangs. You have to let her know she's loved and she's lovable. She doesn't have to be victimized by that. Make sure you let her know that. Build her confidence up so she knows," I said.

"Yeah, I know you're right. I just want to kill him though. I'm going to tell Stephanie. I don't care what she does. His ass done messed with the wrong one this time, buddy, and I'm not having it. I want it out in the open just in case he tries to do it again. Hell, for that matter, Stephanie needs to be careful anyhow 'cause she got all them damn foster kids running around in that damn house. Ain't no telling what's going on up in there. I think they're just using those kids for extra income anyhow," Maysa said as she gulped down a half glass of wine.

"Well, that's a whole different subject. Ummm, I'm almost speechless. Sure, go ahead tell her, but like I said, she's not going to believe you, especially when there's no real proof. Right now, all you have is he said, she said. I'm not even sure you can take that to a court of law. Where's your brother, Olivia's father? I would tell him and let him handle it, man to man. I'm also sure that would take care of it. I know my girls' fathers didn't play about situations like that. They would handle it with a quickness. I didn't need to know the details of it. I just knew it got handled."

"Ms. Bria, girl, you something else. Are you serious?" Maysa asked, wide eyed.

"Like I said, I didn't ask for the details, but neither of my daughters were never, ever bothered again by such nonsense," I answered in a matter-of-fact sort of way and acted like I didn't notice the expression on Maysa's face.

Maysa stood there amazed,   then said, "No, Olivia's father wouldn't be able to handle this situation. His dumb ass would probably want her to take the money so he could get a fix. Naw, but I do know our uncle Juke, my mother's brother, wouldn't play that. He used to run numbers back in the day out of a club in Oak Cliff. Maybe I ought to give him a call, you know? Unfortunately, he's the closest man we have to a father figure."

"Might not be a bad idea. I'm not promoting violence, so don't get me wrong, but some things are better handled man-to -man. The thing is this: That idiot approached Olivia, she said no, so he could say it never happened—like I said, he said, she said. We don't want it to go down like that, but we also don't want him to get away with this perversion. You're just putting it out there that someone other than Olivia knows, and unless he wants to risk the consequences, then oh well, what he gets is what he gets, that's all I'm saying."

"Yeah, that's a thought. I'll give Uncle Juke a call tonight. Better yet, I'mma stop by his crib when I get off. I haven't seen him in a while anyhow. Thanks, girl. You got book sense and street sense. How did someone of your caliber get that thug knowledge?" Maysa asked.

"All I'mma say is I don't look like what I've been through, which hasn't been as bad as some, but it hasn't been as good as others, and I'm going to leave that alone. I just try to live a positive life, treat people kind, stay out of folks' business, find my lane, and run in it. I know my place in this world. So far, that has served me very well. Oh, and might I add, I do have a relationship with the Lord. I might not wear a cross, but trust and believe I do. Did you guys get that car situation taken care of? Sorry for leaving, but once I saw Olivia was alive, I thought I would let you handle your business. I could see how awkward that was for you. I know I've been through enough of those types of situations too. I figured if you really needed some additional help, you'd reach out, and you did when you were ready, so I'm here if you need me."

"Yeah, thank God she was alright and that no train was on the tracks. I just don't know what I nor our family would have done. It could have been so much worse, but the officer who came to the scene was so considerate, saying he had teenagers who had done similar things and that he understood. He was the one who recommended the towing company to get the car off the tracks. So yes, that situation was nothing compared to what she told me about Stephanie's trifling man. Oh, look at the time.

I'd better pull it together. My next appointment will be here soon. Thanks again for all your help, girl," Maysa said.

"No problem, honey. That's what friends are for. Keep me posted on what happens. I need to get back downstairs and get my car moved to the right spot."

At that moment, I heard my text message on my iPhone. It's from Clayton Carter. I forgot I'd saved his contact information in my phone. The message read: Good afternoon, sexy. It was good seeing you this morning. Don't forget to check your schedule. I'm looking forward to seeing you soon. Stay sweet and beautiful.

I just looked at the text, not really knowing how to respond, so I didn't. Interesting, but not yet, Mr. Carter.

"Who's that, girl, a new boo?" Maysa asked.

"Not hardly. No new boo—just some guy I met at the gym. No one to write home about yet. I'm still trying to feel him out. I'm not quite sure how to date at this age anymore. Just can't trust anyone these days, and I'm in no mood for games, so I'm just playing it cool."

"Yeah, well don't think they won't be coming atcha. You have a lot to offer, and I don't mean to sound offensive, but you look pretty damn good for a lady your age. I mean there are some forty-year-old women my age that don't have the body you do. You know what I mean?" Maysa said.

"I know what you mean, and thanks. I'm just trying to live that's all. You know I had a medical scare about a year or so before I retired that kind of put things in a new perspective for me. Then one of my good friends just up and died with no warning as if I didn't already have a lot of stuff on my plate, but then that's life. You just have to roll with it. Anyhow, after all that happened, I decided I had better make better life choices and that included incorporating exercising, healthier eating habits, and a healthier mindset. Long story short, I made some minor and major improvements. I feel good on the inside—that's most important—and I think I look pretty good, no complaints. But girl, yeah, let me get out of here. You and I can talk all day. I just love your energy, and like I said, I'm here for you if you need me. Have a great remainder of your day, and I'll give you a call later tonight."

We both said our goodbyes, hugged, and off I went.

Chapter Ten

IT HAD BEEN A COUPLE days since I had talked with Maysa. To my knowledge, I still hadn't received an actual call from Clayton Carter and I had been checking my voicemail too in case I somehow missed a call from him but no, yet that hadn't stopped his daily text messages. I was a little curious. I hadn't run into him at the gym the last few times I was there, but I downplayed it by acting like it hadn't mattered to me that I hadn't seen him and kept it moving. I ran it down to Suni who thought it was okay for women to call men. She said it was the thing to do nowadays.

Suni said, "Women can be forward, Bria. Hell, it's a different game out there now."

But me, I'm still old school. Like Steve Harvey said, I, too, am of the adage men are hunters. They go after what they want.

I think about all the men from my past I thought I couldn't live without who for whatever reason I pursued, and it didn't work out. In retrospect, some of them I know today, and I'm glad it didn't work out. Whew, thank you, Lord. It's for that reason I've learned not to force relationships. I don't expect any man to give me what he's incapable of giving. Some men simply don't have the capacity to meet certain expectations. I've learned to get in tune with my inner intuition and know when to say no, when to let go, and when to move on. But just to have a little fun, I was looking forward to hearing from Mr. Carter. Not so sure I'll call him though, he knew how to reach me, I had made sure of that so I decided to wait.

"Girl, call the fuckin' man. It ain't gonna kill you," was the response from Suni when we were on the phone catching up from the last couple of days. Suni knows she has a way with words. I don't ever have to worry about her holding back.

"Girl, I'm just following his lead, taking my time. If its meant to be, he'll call if not oh well. But I'm not calling him yet, my mind is made up about that. The ball is in his court, besides that was our agreement." I said.

"And how do you know he's not following your lead? Didn't you say he looked like he was in his mid -sixties? Well hell, you gon' wait too long, and there won't be any need to worry about his old ass. I'm just saying, at least call him and see what he's about. Meet him somewhere public, go out for coffee—drinks, something—just pick a mutual spot. I know I would," Suni said.

"I know you would. You don't have any fear in that regard. I'm still trying to weigh my options. I'm trying to get the courage to go on one of the dating sites. Girl, I guess I'm just too cautious."

"Naw. Your ass ain't that damn cautious, not the way you used to take off whenever you got those booty texts from that Fav as you called him. I don't know what your problem is, but how are you going to meet people when you won't even give the guy that's right in your face a chance? For me, I haven't met anyone interesting in person other than the guys I've met on the dating sites. Now, I will say, some haven't worked out, but I've gained some lasting friends from going on that site, too, so it hasn't been all bad. You just weed out the bad ones and keep it moving. But you know me, I ain't trying to get with no man who acts older and has more health challenges than me. I'm passed that stage,   and my age range is forty-five to fifty-five," Suni said.

"Girl, you're crazy, I can't believe you would seriously date a man ten to twenty years younger than you. What the hell do I look like with some man five or six years younger than me? It's been so long, I don't know if my stuff still works." I laughed.

"Well, yes ma'am I would, believe it, my stuff still works, and while it's working, I want something to work with it. I don't want someone who I have to prime and whatever to stay awake or who's on all kinds of medication that his stuff don't get hard or his ass passes out after he comes one time or who might even defecate on me."

"Suni, whaaat? Oh my God, girl, what did you just say? Defecate as in shit on you?" I couldn't believe my friend. She was so out of control, but I loved her to death.

"Yeah. Well, that's a whole different story. Remind me to tell you about that one day. It would be one thing had I been married to the guy for some years and had to accept my husband's condition based on the 'in sickness and health' disclaimer in the marriage vows, but I'm not married, and since I'm not, I prefer a well-able-bodied man. That's my preference, and I'm sticking to it," Suni said.

"I hear ya, and I'm glad you're a woman who knows what she wants and isn't afraid to say so. On another subject, how did your appointment go?" I asked Suni.

She acted like she hadn't heard one word of my question and kept ranting on.

"Girl, yes, I'm firm about what and who I want 'cause some of them are just played out old Casanovas that are looking for someone to play nurse, house maid, caregiver, and so on. I ain't trying to be that domesticated. So yeah, you got to be careful," Suni surmised.

"I get it, I get it. Now again I asked, and don't act like you don't hear me, heifer. How did your last checkup go? Is everything alright?" I managed to say to her.

"Well, yes and no. As they say, I have good news and bad news. Which one do you want first?" Suni asked.

"Look, don't play with me, girl. Tell me what's going on. Do I need to book a flight now or what?"

"My gynecologist identified a spot on my mammogram results. Long story short, she referred me to an oncologist. The good news is my pap smear was good this time. Since that ovarian cancer scare a few years ago, I couldn't take another episode like that again. Lord knows I don't know if I even have the strength."

"Okay, so when were you going to say something about this, Suni? You know I'm here for you," I said.

"Yeah, I know. I just didn't want you to worry. Even though you've been in your new location almost two years, it seems like you just relocated . I know it takes time to get acclimated to new surroundings, your own annual appointments and schedules and what have you. The last thing I want you to be doing is worrying about what's going on with me. You have your new life ahead of you. My sister has been very supportive, believe me. I've been okay. I know you would be with me if you were here, I will always appreciate you being with me through my journey with the ovarian cancer. I'll never forget that. This is just another part of life and things that come up in it, I'll be alright," Suni said.

"Well, don't be so cavalier about it, Suni. When will you get the results from the spot on the breast? I'm a bit concerned you're already seeing an oncologist. There's more, isn't there?" I asked.

"You have that mother wit that can't nobody fool you, Bria. Yes, there's more. It's just that based on my family history, there's a high likelihood I have breast cancer, but there's also a high likelihood they can remove the breast and I'm all good. The thing is after my ovarian cancer, I had the genetic test that determined my BRCA gene was positive and in the eighty percentile range. That means the chances of me getting breast cancer are very high. You know my mother had cancer, and so did her sister. Anytime you or another one of your immediate blood relatives have been diagnosed, you should have the genetic mutations test. That's why I did it, and so did my sister. I just believe the Lord didn't bring me this far to leave me. I'm trusting that, and I've already prayed about it. I've decided to have both breasts removed. Hell, I need bigger ones anyhow, so I ain't tripping. I've already researched it. After the surgery, they put in what they call expanders until you reach your desired size. Over a period of time—I think every week, or something like that—I'll go in for a regular visit then they'll check me out, and once I'm where I want to be, they'll schedule me for the silicone implants. Modern medicine has come a long way from where it was years ago, so I believe I'll be alright," Suni said.

"Wow. That's a lot for me to process, Suni. You never cease to amaze me, my friend. You are a beast at survival. I admire your courage and strength and the humor you take it all in with," I said.

"Girl, you know I talk a lot of shit. I'm the first to admit it, but when it comes to faith and knowing where my help comes from, you know I don't play. I know God's got this and this too shall pass," Suni said.

"Yes, ma'am, I agree. This is just another one of life's pauses, trying to catch you off balance and knock you off your square. You're too strong for that. I know it, and you're right, God's got you. You just make sure you keep me in the loop and let me know when and where and what the outcome is. I'm not playing with you either. Don't make me come to Rockford and kick your ass," I said.

Good thing we were on the phone because by the end of our call I had teared up. We each said our I love yous and were off the phone.

I had to pull it together. I knew I had to be positive for Suni's sake and mine too for that matter. After the sudden death of my good friend Lynette Cummings from back in the day, I dreaded the inevitable news of something terrible happening to any of my loved ones. I was grateful to have had a genuine and loyal circle of friends. We had been there for one another over the years, and it meant a lot. With my girlfriend network, there was a tight bond and closeness because we chose to be friends based on our compatibility. You don't choose your family, so with that being said, when you have a sisterhood like ours, you cherished it and held it tightly. My small network of girlfriends meant a lot to me.

Chapter Eleven

THE LAST FEW DAYS HAD been like a whirlwind. My mind had been so consumed with what Maysa and Suni were going through that I almost forgot to call Harmony and wish her and Jamal happy anniversary. I think I made a post on her Facebook page, but I liked to reach out and talk. I picked up my phone, and I saw another text from Clayton. I also noticed I'd been getting a lot of missed unknown caller ID numbers lately. Clayton's message was the typical Good morning, sexy. How are you today? Stay beautiful. Miss you.

This guy is acting so mysterious, we've spoken only casually during a couple of our visits at the gym, yet he'll send me text messages saying miss you, but has yet to call me. I can't figure that one out. Oh well. I didn't respond to the text messages. I'm done with text relationships. But I don't know who these unknown calls are from. The next time I get one, I think I'll answer just for the sake of it, especially since I knew it couldn't be a bill collector as all my bills are paid and on time. I'm done with those days, too, thank God.

I looked as I heard the ringtone of my iPhone, and coincidentally, I see it's an unknown call. How amazing is it that I've been waiting on this. Oh well, here goes.

"Hello," I answered.

"Hey, beautiful. How are you? I finally caught you," a very familiar voice said.

"Really? Well, may I ask who I'm speaking with?" I asked.

"It hasn't been that long since we last talked. This is Clayton. You gon' act like you don't know my voice by now, honey? I would've thought you'd be expecting my call." Clayton said.

"I guess I'm taken aback since I haven't had the pleasure of speaking with you on the phone. It's a wonder I even answered your call being that it comes up as unknown caller. Why is that?" I asked, thinking, How in the hell would I recognize your voice? You act like you and I talk regularly. What an asshole.

"Well, that's just how I have my service set up. So now you know anytime you see that, just answer the call. It's me."

"That's odd and very peculiar. Are you aware you gave me your number to call you and that when you text your name appears on my end because I saved your name and number to my Contact list? So why is it you don't want your identity known when you call, Clayton? Like I said, I find that a bit strange. You must have something to hide. I'm not in the habit of answering unknown calls. The only reason I answered this time was out of curiosity since I noticed I had been receiving so many lately," I said.

"Well, my dear, I don't have anything to hide. That's just the way I have my calls set up. It's been like that for the past fifteen years or so. Anyhow, if you're done chastising me about my phone, I was calling to ask if you'd like to join me for breakfast, lunch, or brunch soon, I've given you more than enough time to check your schedule." he stated.

"How do you define soon? I have a couple of things going on, so it depends on when you're talking about." I answered.

"How's tomorrow, is that too soon for you? I already know you're an early riser from the times I've ran into you at the gym. So how about you and I skip the gym tomorrow and go have a nice breakfast somewhere?"

And before I could stop myself, I heard me say, "Sure. Where and what time? I'll meet you."

When I hung up, I remembered I had better call Harm before I let time get away from me. I tabbed to my recent call list, scrolled for Girlfriend, and tapped.

"Hey. How are you?" Harmony asked.

"Hey, gurrl. I'm good. I just wanted to call and say happy anniversary to the best couple I know. I'm not going to keep you long. I know you guys always have plans, so let bro-n-law know I love him and the girls too," I said.

"Why thank you. Yeah, we're going to dinner later tonight. We're both working today. What's been happening with you? Suni said you met a man," Harmony said.

"Suni knows she couldn't hold water if her life depended on it. Yeah, I met one. I'm still not too sure about him, which was why I hadn't said anything yet," I said.

I proceeded to catch Harmony up on all the details about Clayton from the initial meeting up to our recent phone call. "So, what do you think?" I asked.

"Well, he doesn't exactly sound like your type, but then again, you don't want to pigeonhole yourself without giving the guy a chance. It is weird he calls as unknown caller. I mean, what's up with that? Is he a celebrity or something? I doubt that 'cause he gave you his card and information. I'll tell you what, make sure you let somebody know where you're going so someone knows."

"I definitely will, so that's that. I was thinking about going on that ChristiansMeet.com website."

"Now, I'm totally against that. I worked with a lady that got hooked up on one of those sites, and it was an absolute mess. Turns out the guy was a fraud and scammed her out of all kinds of money. I don't recommend you doing that. I've heard of women who've had too many bad experiences," Harmony said.

"Yeah. I've heard both sides. I don't know, I just know dating isn't what it used to be. Anyhow, I've got to run and so do you, so we'll catch up later. Enjoy your evening. We'll talk soon," I replied.

The next morning, I was up feeling both trepidation and anticipation, and after my morning routine of showering and performing my skincare and using Bath and Body Works body lotion of essential oils and shea butter ritual, I dressed in a casual pair of Zella leggings along with a coordinating oversized long-sleeve tuck-front t-shirt, a pair of bootie socks and Nikes. I grabbed my purse and iPhone, and next thing you know, I was driving out on Interstate 35 East, headed to meet Clayton for our get-acquainted breakfast. Based on my navigation system, my exit was about a fourth of a mile down the road to the right.

Just as I was about to find a park, my phone rang. From the screen, all I saw was Call, No Name. I hit the answer.

"Hello," I said.

"Good morning. How far out are you?" Clayton asked.

"As a matter of fact, I'm here now, just parking. How about you? Where are you?"

"I see you. I'm in that SLC 300 Roadster Mercedes Benz to the far left. I'll wait for you. We can walk in together," Clayton said.

"Oh, okay. I see you now."

Boy, how could I not see him? I thought. Must have been a Texas thing because what I saw was a black man with a large cowboy hat, casual wear, and what looked like snakeskin or crocodile cowboy boots, but I didn't let that deter me. I tried to keep an open mind, ignoring the first signs of flashiness—the red Nike apparel and the Mercedes Benz ring from the gym, now the car and his outfit . My thought process at this point was, Let's just get through this and be done, so into the restaurant we went.

Clayton actually wasn't a bad-looking man for his age. I could see he must have been attractive in his day. He welcomed me with open arms, a wide smile, and a hug. We made idle chit-chat walking into the building and during the intervals of being waited on and served, then during breakfast. I noticed Clayton was overly friendly with the waitstaff and other customers in the establishment. I couldn't quite put my finger on whether that too was a southern thing or just his overconfidence, so I ignored it. I just wasn't in the habit of being that overindulging of strangers, so I looked at it as being our difference in personalities. I was really trying to be openminded.

Through the course of our time together, Clayton said he was retired military and had a second career as a college professor from which he had also retired. He said he was divorced and was now living alone in Texas because of the cost of living. He felt Texas had a lot to offer retirees. Clayton said he lived in one of the neighboring towns where not many blacks lived, but from the sounds of it, and based on what I knew, there was hardly any place anymore that African Americans couldn't afford to live if and when they chose. I didn't know what he meant by making that comment. He sounded like someone who wasn't used to anything as my momma would say. I ignored it, not wanting to debate, so I just let him ramble. Before we were done, I managed to tell him a little about myself—where I was from, what I did in my past life, my divorce, not looking for anything, only get to know yous as I was not ready for love and relationship nor was I interested in sleeping around. I had to make that clear since as he put it, we are grown folks. I glanced at my Apple Watch and told him I had an appointment and I should get going. After Clayton got the attention of the server, we wrapped things up and strolled out.

As we approached our cars, I noticed someone had parked right next to Clayton's small Mercedes. I noticed a slight change in Clayton's demeanor by the expression on his face and the increased pace in his stride as he approached his vehicle. I thought he was going to lose it. Instead he said, "I don't care how far out you park, all these open spaces, somebody always wants to park right next to you."

"Yep, you're right. Looks like they're still in the car. I don't even know how they're going to get out of that vehicle as close as it's parked next to you. Looks like you'd better handle that," I responded.

The car was so close, I couldn't believe my own eyes. I said goodbye, thanks for breakfast—the typical pleasantries—and hurried to my car. I knew Clayton had other business at hand, and I didn't want him to worry about me.

Clayton tried to refocus, gave me a hug, said he'd call me soon, and he scurried along toward his vehicle. I looked in my rearview mirror as I left and saw he was near the driver's side of the car next to his speaking to whomever was in it. I then saw two white women get out of the car. I didn't bother to slow poke around for what was next. That was his business. I made it a habit not to get in other folk's affairs, and I was out.

Chapter Twelve

LATER THAT SAME DAY, I received a call from Clayton explaining how he had to help the woman in the vehicle next to his park her car correctly and how he had jokingly said to her, "You parked your car like my girlfriend," somehow insinuating I was his girlfriend.

I ignored that comment. I let him know again I appreciated the breakfast and said thank you. He went on as if we were actually dating, and he wanted to know what my plans were later in the day. I cut the call short and said I had an appointment and would talk to him some other time. Again, I thought, must be a southern thing, maybe even a Texas thing, him appearing to be moving too fast, being too intrusive. I wasn't sure, but what I did know was I wasn't feeling his vibe. Something was off with him. Was he pleasant? Yes. Did he make me laugh? Yes. Was I flattered? Absolutely. But still, there was something not quite up to par with him.

My appointment wasn't really an appointment, rather it was me wanting to do whatever it was I needed to do or wanted to do at my leisure, which was stop by Target and grab a few things I wanted to pick up in anticipation of India and Shea's visit, then I wanted to drive out to Maysa's salon to see how things were going and to also let her know about my so-called date with Clayton. I got out there around one, so Maysa had some free time to chitchat for a bit. I gave her the play-by -play rundown on Clayton, which led up to our breakfast and how I felt there was something I couldn't quite put my finger on.

"Have you looked him up on Facebook yet?"

"Believe it or not, that's one of the first things I did, but he isn't on Facebook. I even called myself Googling him, but I couldn't really find any information," I said.

"You know what, sounds like the man is married. That's what a lot of these Texas guys do. See, you can't be too careful nowadays. Some of them think they can have a chick in town after town because it's so large here. You been out the game too long, Ms. Bria."

"What, you don't think he would be so bold as to ask me to breakfast and what-not in broad daylight if he's married, do you? I mean, really? I don't mean to sound naïve, but I would think he's too old for that type of foolishness," I said.

"Okay, so what's his last name, and where does he live? We're going to do some detective work on him. There's more than one way. First, we're going to do a search on fastpeoplesearch.com, which will give us some free information and something to go on. There are tons of ways we can get information on people today, and trust and believe, I know how to do it. If that doesn't give us what we need to know, I know another way, but we might not have to use that. Let's see what we got," Maysa said.

"Dammmnnn," I said in my Janet Jackson voice. "It pays to have a younger woman as a friend these days—help an old girl out, sista."

I gave Maysa all the information she needed. Maysa pulled out her laptop and started typing in fastpeoplesearch.com, and wouldn't you know it? She inputted Clayton's first and last name along with the city and state. His information came up. The screen displayed the area he lived in. We got his birthday, home address, names of potential family members, and particularly a woman with the same last name. Maysa went so far as searching the property records of the address on a different site and found the home he lived in was in the same woman's name identified in Fast People Search.

Maysa then searched Facebook under the woman's name and saw her Facebook profile was a picture of her and guess who? Mr. Clayton himself. The pictures were posted on a recent date. Clayton might have been divorced at one time, but from the appearance of the picture, he was remarried and to a much younger woman. I had been duped.

"There you have it. So, whatcha gon' do with this info, girl? We got to think about this. You know I watch a lot of Dateline and stuff. I saw one show where a woman found out a man she had been dating was lying to her and had a whole wife and family. He killed her when she approached him with the information, so girl, I think you ought to just let him go, tell him you're not interested, and let that be it. You don't want him to think you're trying to wreck what he already got, you know what I mean?" Maysa said.

"Yeah, I do, and at the same time I don't want to get caught up in some man's indiscretions with his wife like I'm his side-piece or whatever. He has to be crazy for putting me in harms way by meeting me publicly or is it the fact that the metroplex is so large that he presumed he could have an affair with me or whomever and get away with it. Whatever his game was he chose the wrong one, I surely don't want anyone accusing me of their husband or any nonsense like that. But the nerve of that old bastard. What makes him think I want to be fooling around with someone's husband? It just makes me angry to think he was trying to play me like that. It must be a lot of superficial women around here for him to think I was one of them. Flashing his Mercedes emblems and car around me like that, talking about how much money he has and how he travels, trying to impress me with that nonsense. What nerve. But you're right, I need to process how I'm going to handle all this. I won't go out of my way to confront him with it. I'll just wait until I hear from him again, then I'm pretty sure I'll let him have it. We'll see. Thanks for all your help, Maysa. See, this is the type of stuff that makes me sick. You just don't know who to trust anymore. It's this type of thing that gives all good men a bad break," I said.

"You're in the big state of Texas, honey. Yes, there are lots of superficial people here, men and women. Don't get me wrong, there are some good people here, too—good men specifically. Personally, I know some couples who are in very trustworthy and lasting relationships, but, unfortunately, there are some girls and women who all they want is a sugar daddy type to, one, get their hair and nails done and two, buy them a Louis Vuitton bag, pay a car note or rent, put a little change in their pocket and that's it. Sometimes these guys see you and prey on your type 'cause they think you like nice things so you'll settle for any means necessary to get those things, even if it means being that side chick. It's like anything else in life: You have to weed out the bad and know the difference. It doesn't matter what your age bracket is, it's the game, baby," Maysa said.

"Well, excuse my vernacular, but I ain't about that life and whatever nice things I like, have, or get, I work hard for. I'm not—and I can't stress enough, not—interested in foolery. I'm darn near sixty and not trying to be part of no man's harem of women. Thank God I'm above where I used to be. Sleeping around with a guy is not my M.O. I want respect. In fact, I demand it. I remember a time when, I'm ashamed to admit it, but by the time this type of news got to me, I was knee deep in sex and emotions too far gone to make any sound judgment," I said.

"Yeah, well you weren't the only one. That's a lot of our problem today. We allow sex to be the driving factor in relationships. That's why many of us are in bad ones," Maysa said.

"Yeah, you're right. So, how's the situation with Olivia? Did you say anything to Stephanie yet?" I asked.

"No, I didn't. You know this has been hard for me to process. What that punk did was clearly wrong. He had no business making a pass at my niece. Nothing—and I mean nothing— excuses that, but I promise I'll protect Olivia with everything in me. I'll make sure nothing ever happens to her while she's under my care. I'm glad she knows she can trust me and confide in me. Me and my mom had a long talk with her,   and I let her know she can count on me to be there for her and so did my mother and other immediate family members. I don't want her to feel like she has to take matters into her own hands like that poor Cyntoia Brown ordeal. Lord knows that was a horror story. I want Olivia to be aware of men out there who only have one purpose, and that's to use and abuse women. He will get his. It's just too bad there are women like Stephanie who help perpetuate this type of foolishness because they waste time with men like that," Maysa said.

"I agree with you on that. I can't for the life of me believe some of what goes on in today's society and has been going on for so long. This is the type of stuff we've just swept under the rug for far too long. I know women who have stayed in relationships and who knew their husbands or significant others were doing this, that, or the other, but for the sake of having a piece of a man as my mama would say, stayed with the man. I guess I'll never have one if I have to settle for that crap. Not to mention the trauma it causes to children, male and female. Some women do put their men before their children. That's sad too. The children didn't ask to be here, you know? But some women just bring man after man after man in and around their children. No wonder there are so many confused and traumatized youth out here today. Oh well, enough of my tangent. I'm just glad Olivia is alright and you, too, 'cause I thought you were going to kill somebody," I said.

"Girl, naw, I just needed to get myself together. I'm cool. So, are you all set for your daughters' visit? When are they coming?" Maysa said.

"Yes. I'm getting excited and can't wait to see them. They'll be here in a couple more weeks. I think I'll set up spa appointments with Isla's team for us too. They'll enjoy that. I'd better get going. We'll talk later."

Chapter Thirteen

IT WAS SATURDAY AT FIVE o'clock a.m., and I was wide awake. I was still unsettled about how I was going to handle Mr. Clayton. A few days had passed since I last spoke with him, but the unknown calls hadn't ceased. I was annoyed by them and had decided to use that feature on my iPhone to block a caller. The only problem was Mr. Clayton's unknown caller ID calls still came through. The feature only prevented me from receiving his text messages since I had saved his contact information. No more. I decided I had to address this—and soon. This man had no right to trespass my territory with his deception. Seems as soon as I made up my mind to deal with him and take his next call, the calls stopped coming. I guess he got the message. I was still outraged, but like anything else, I'd get over it.

Maybe Maysa was right. The more I thought about it, going after him with the disclosure might not be in my best interest. My thoughts were interrupted by my iPhone ringing. I looked in the direction of the sound to reach for my device, which was on my nightstand. By the area code, I could tell it was a call from Illinois. I was somewhat alarmed whenever I received an early morning or late-night call because I would expect the worst news, especially since my children were in Illinois. Even though I had their contact information saved, a call from home could mean someone else was calling to give me bad news about one of them. So, without any hesitation I answered it.

"Hello," I spoke into the phone.

"Hello, Bria. Hope this isn't a bad time. This is Lance. How are you?"

"Lance? Lance Townsend?"

"Yes. How many other Lances do you know? Has it been that long?"

"Since you put it that way, yes, it has been that long. I'm good, Lance. What's going on? Is everything alright?"

"Yes, everything is fine. I was just thinking about you and thought I would give my friend a call to see how things were going for you. I ran into one of our mutual friends from school who said you had moved to Dallas, Texas. I have a business trip coming up in a few weeks and was wondering if you'd like to do dinner or something," Lance said.

"Really...and who was that?"

"Juanita."

"Oh, wow. I haven't talked to her in I don't know when. That's interesting."

"Anyhow, I wanted to catch you early so you could pencil me on your schedule. I would really like to see you."

"Are you kidding me, Lance? Aren't you still married? Why on God's green earth would I want to go out to dinner with someone's husband? No thank you. It was nice to hear from you, but no, I don't think that's a good idea at all. Good day, brotha, and please don't bother to call my number again, not unless you're bringing your wife." I hung up.

What the hell was that all about? I thought. Lance Townsend was a guy from way back in my past whom I thought I couldn't live without, but as time would have it, I did. Lance and I never really had much of a relationship. It was one of those things in between Leon and Omar, sometime after I had Zach as a teenager. Lance was good looking, on the high school basketball team, but I guess he didn't want a readymade family, so our so-called relationship never materialized. He would often come back home after his high school graduation and thought he and I could hook up whenever he wanted. Truth be told, I did because I was so freaking crazy about him. But that was then. The nerve of him now. Some things just never change.

I wasn't sure what or who he thought I was now. My past was just that, my past. I wasn't the same vulnerable naïve lovestruck little girl. For the second time, my thoughts were interrupted by the sound of my iPhone's ring tone. I looked and it was the same number.

"Yes, may I help you?" I spoke harshly into the phone.

"Bria, please don't hang up. I know it seems unusual me call-ing and all, but believe me, I just want you to hear what I have to say. I wanted to say it to you in person. Please hear me out. Would you do that for me, please?" Lance said.

By now, he had my full attention, and I was sitting straight up in my bed fearful of what he had to say that was so important for me to hear.

"Okay, so what is it, Lance?" I said.

"Over the last several years, I've been doing some soul searching. I want to apologize for the way I treated you way back when we were seeing each other. I never intended to hurt you in any way, shape, or form. It was just that I saw something in you that I just couldn't handle. You didn't even see it in your-self. You were always so strong and in some ways kind of intim-idating. I knew I wasn't the one for you, so I chose to leave you. But after all these years, I still think of our friendship and what it really meant to me. I remember some of our conversations. You always had that mother's wit. Even at a young age, you were so full of wisdom and knowledge. So, what I'm saying to you now is you're a very special person. I've kept up with you from a distance. I know you're ambitious—you always have been—and I want you to know I support you, and I'm here for you. If you ev-er need anything, don't hesitate to call me. I don't mean that in any funny way. I have no ulterior motive. I want you to be en-couraged and know there's someone here who has your back. That's all I wanted to share with you. You'll always be my forev-er friend. No matter what, I trust you, and I want you to trust me. Whether we have dinner face-to-face or not, I had to let you know that."

"Are you okay, Lance?" I asked.

"Yes, I'm fine. Like I said, I needed to let you know that. I'm not trying to come on to you. I made a vow to my wife, and I promised to uphold that vow to God, to her, and to my family. But my conscience needed to be clear, so I needed to speak with you."

"Thank you. I appreciate your apology. I guess there was a time when I thought I wasn't good enough for you, which was why I presumed things hadn't worked out between us. I mean, I got over it, but thanks. I don't know what else to say. I'm glad all is well with you. I'm good. I've had a lot of years to process events from my past, and I thank God for all of it. I realize I wouldn't be the person I am today had it not been for my previous experiences, so I have no regrets," I said.

"Bria, thank you for hearing me out. It means a lot to me, and I mean it. Remember, if you ever need anything, don't hesitate to let me know," Lance said.

"I'll take what you said into consideration. You don't owe me anything. It was nice hearing from you, Lance. Take care," I said and ended the call.

Chapter Fourteen

I LOVED THE SMELL AND look of fresh flowers indoors, so I made it a point to pick up a bunch whenever I went to the market. Now even more so since I wanted to create an inviting ambiance for my daughters. I went to Bath and Body Works and picked up a few items to make each one a special gift basket as well as make them each a spa towel set. Even though they were coming to their second home to visit me, I wanted to make sure they each felt special. They were both grown, but they were still my babies. I couldn't wait to see Shea and India. We had so much fun together. India had made sure she sent me their updated itinerary, which denoted an arrival time into DFW airport on Thursday at 2:34 p.m., which meant we would have all day

Friday, Saturday, and Sunday before their early departure on Monday morning.

It was going to be like old times, just me and the girls. Not that it wasn't great when all of us got together—Zach and my grandchild—but our girl time togetherness reminded me of the good old days when India, Shea, and I would laugh and play in makeup, discuss clothes, and girl chitchat. Now that they were older, I enjoyed getting their perspectives about life. Seems the girl power movement was fierce and bolder with the younger generation. These young women knew what they wanted out of life and didn't let anything or anybody stand in their way of getting it. They encouraged me, which is why I valued Maysa's relationship so much. Being around young intelligent minds helped propel, fuel, and recharge me.

I checked my weather app on my iPhone to see the forecast would be in the nineties and sunny for the next few days. Perfect, I thought. Outside of our spa treatments, I planned to take the girts to see the heart of the north DFW metroplex. I knew they didn't particularly care for the sports scene, but they and even I would get a kick out of seeing that massive AT&T stadium where the Dallas Cowboys played, as well as the new Globe Life Field of the Texas Rangers. At night, both looked very impressive and inviting. Also, on my to-do list for them was Texas Live! From what I heard, it was a cool spot to walk around, people watch, and enjoy the scenery. Also on my list was Lo Lo's Chicken and Waffles and a few other local-owned spots that had been recommended for us to see. Based on the list I had, we might not get to all, but at least we had some things to consider doing without running the risk of getting bored. Besides, everything on my list was within a fifteen- to twenty-minute radius for us to get to. We could easily Lyft or Uber to get to our destinations without being bothered with driving and parking restrictions. Ultimately, I decided I would let them figure out what they wanted to do. India always said I didn't know how to relax, so this time I would show her I do and that I don't have to be in control of everything. My ideas would only be presented as rec-ommendations—whatever they wanted. I had made up my mind to roll with the flow. I was simply glad they were coming.

Hours later, I was ready to wind down. I lit some candles, had a glass of wine, and ran a bath with essential oils to help me relax before I retired for the evening. When morning came, I would skip the gym but take a brisk walk through the neighbor-hood for three to four miles. I still had time to get a shower and freshen up since the girls' flight was after two, and it only took me fifteen minutes or so to get to DFW airport.

It seemed no sooner had I fallen into the REM stage of sleep, I was awakened by the ringtone on my phone. I looked first to see the time. It was eight forty-six. I saw the name and face of the caller. It was my friend Connie.

"I woulda thought you'd be up and at 'em already. Sounds like you're still sleeping. So what time are you picking up the girls today?" Connie asked.

"I know, I'm usually up before now, you're right. Their plane arrives at two-thirty-four, so I'll leave home around two. It'll only take me fifteen minutes to get to the airport," I responded.

As it turned out, Connie had just phoned to check in and to give me an update on the plans for our next girlfriends trip to Jamaica. I was accustomed to Connie's early-morning phone calls.   She and I usually spoke first thing in the morning because we were both typically early risers; Suni and Harmony were just the opposite.

"Okay, so you have a little time then. Did you get that information I sent you about the resort? I emailed it to you. I want you to look it over before I send it out to Suni and Harm. We know how picky you are about hotels."

"Girl, I trust your judgment. Why don't you set up a conference call, and we can all discuss it then? But do it after my long weekend with India and Shea. That'll give me something to look forward to after they leave," I said.

"Sounds like your retired behind has been quite busy if you ask me, and speaking of being busy, Suni said you met a man?" Connie asked.

"Wow. People sure have been talking, haven't they?" I said, laughing.

"Girl, you know Suni can't hold nothing. She told me all about it. No worries, catch me up, so what's that man business about. Have you heard from him anymore?"

"No, I haven't. I stopped taking the unknown calls, and I blocked him in my phone, which means I no longer get his text messages, if he even texts. But that won't stop him from calling unknown, you know what I mean?" I said.

"Yes, I do. If it was me though, I'd take his call and let his ass know I knew. Trifling bastard. Tie up those lose ends, girl. I would let him have it."

"I thought about it, but anyhow, the calls have stopped, and I'm not going out of my way to speak to him. He's not that important to me. But I hear what you're saying, and if he ever calls,

I'll be sure to answer and let him know I peeped his card. How's everything with you and the family?" I said.

"So far, so good, except we might have to take in my mother-in-law. Sounds like her dementia is getting real bad, and no one else in the family wants to step up to the plate, so I told Chad whatever he thinks is best, I'll support it," Connie said.

"Wow, that's major for you, isn't it? Especially since you weren't exactly on her list of favorite people over the years. I guess it's true what they say: Be careful how you treat people, huh?" I said.

"I know, right? They betta be glad I love Chad, that's all I know. Anyhow, girl, take a look at the information I sent, enjoy the visit with your girls, and be on the lookout for an invite to our next girlfriends conference call so we can all go over the details, like deposits and so forth," Connie said.

"Sure will. We'll talk soon."

Soon as we ended the call, it dawned on me I had forgotten to mention the unexpected call I received from Lance. Oh well. I made a mental note and a physical note in my notebook to remind myself to discuss with the girlfriends on our next conference call.

Chapter Fifteen

THE TIME WITH INDIA AND Shea came and went so fast. We didn't do much of anything I had planned. India wanted to just chill, so we spent most of our time together hanging around my condo complex. Of course we did shop, went to Lo Lo's Chicken and Waffles, visited North Park Mall, and had lunch. One evening, Shea cooked for us because she wanted to show off her culinary skills from the school she had been attending in Wisconsin. The girls had agreed to allow me to show them off, so we did go to the spa for our treatments, and I introduced them to Maysa, Mona, and Isla. India and Mona had a lot in common since I found out India was intrigued with the spa industry and wanted to know more about skincare and the business of it all. From what I could make out, it sounded like India might even consider a business trip back to the area to get more hands-on detail. That was news to me. Nonetheless, I was happy to hear it, but I didn't want to let on.

Shea ended up going out with some of her school friends from back home who had relocated to the Dallas area and had spent a day touring the city with them and hanging out. All in all, their visit was good, and on the last night, we ended up spending some quality time together, I drank my favorite pinot grigio, India drank her red merlot, and Shea drank Remy on the rocks. The night before their departure, we stayed up late and played a game of home Family Feud with Alexa in the background playing Jill Scott Radio.

"Come on, y'all. We might as well play a game of Family Feud and make this night fun," Shea said.

"It's only fun when there's a whole group of us playing. It's only three of us. How much fun can that be?" India asked.

"Aw, girl, come on. Stop being a party pooper. I'll be the announcer, and you and Mom can answer the questions. You in, Mom?" Shea asked.

"Why not? Let's go for it," I said.

"Mom, did you ever give any more thought to online dating? I thought we were supposed to be setting up an account for you. I think you should give it a try. At least see what kind of hits you get," India said.

"Yeah. It might give you some extra-curricular activities to do. You just never know Mom. I mean what else have you got going on, it's not like you're getting hits from anyone," Shea said, barely audible while setting up the game cards.

"I mean, I get it. I want her to take hits. I mean if she didn't, she'd be a freakin' terrorist around here," India said.

I screamed.

"*Ummm,* I'm sitting right here. You guys are talking about me as if I'm not in the room. Hello. Are you kidding me? And what does 'taking or getting hits mean?" I said.

"Mom, come on, you know...ok so what I mean is, has anyone tried to get your attention by showing you they like you or are interested in you. Same as what your generation would imply as a man hitting on a woman. No. I'm dead serious. I mean, pleasure yourself or something, geez," India said.

"India, TMI. I don't want to hear about Mom and what you're talking about," Shea said.

"Shea, get over it. How in the world do you think you got here? Anyway, there's nothing wrong with online dating. Mom, bring your laptop. I think we should hook you up," India said.

"Well, come to find out, Suni has been doing it for years, and it worked for her," I said.

"*Hmmph.* It did. Well, where are they now?" India said.

"You know, that's a good question. I don't know. I guess it didn't work out, but I don't know why," I said.

"Well, hell, I can answer that. If it has anything to do with the way she talks around us, it's evident. She's scared the good ones off," India said.

Shea was steadily busying herself with the Family Feud game pieces, which I knew couldn't be taking that long. That was just her way of not being in the conversation. That was how Shea was—she downplayed everything while India was the outspoken one.

"What? I'm surprised at you saying that, India. Then again, you could be right. I mean women have to have something to bring to the table too. I could never understand us women who always want a good man, but immediately talk about what can you do for me. A man shouldn't be your financial or retirement plan. Now me, on the other hand, I guess I can take that to the extreme level, huh?" I said.

"*Ummm,* yes, mother dear. You do. You be like, 'Partner, I got this. I got my own money, crib, car... I'm good. I don't need you for that.' Yeah, so you might want to lighten up a bit, tone that down just a tad bit...I'm just saying, Mom. No disrespect. I mean you out here like, 'Damn, I don't need a man.' Excuse the profanity, Mom, but don't miss the message. I'm just saying," India said.

"Let's just play the game, India. You can't fix nobody. First question: Name something that makes you know you've found the right one. Mom, you go first," Shea spoke.

"Wait, let me be the reader. You and mom answer the questions," India said.

"Whatever, girl. Here, go for it," Shea said and passed the cards to India.

"Chemistry, communication," I said.

"Nope. Shea..."

"Finances, brains," Shea said.

"Nope. Bong," India said.

"Y'all both are wrong and y'all are cheating 'cause you're supposed to give one answer at a time, but I gave you a pass on that. The answers are heart flutters, can't stop thinking about the other person, happiness, makes laugh, butterflies in stomach, smile... See, sounds to me like that's the problem. Women don't even know what the relationship triggers are. You guys are answering superficial things that you want and not what's important in relationships. Like I said, maybe, just maybe, that's the issue here. As far as the topic of relationships goes, y'all haven't received any points. I'm done," India said.

"Girl, are you kidding me? You're too much," I said.

"I hope both of you are better at relationships in real life than you were at answering these questions 'cause if I had to judge from this game, you ladies have a lot of work to do. How'd you guys come up with the answers you gave? Mom, come on you've got to brush up your skills, girl. Seriously?" India joked.

"Girl, it was just a game. It's not that serious," Shea said.

"No, it is that serious, Shea. Mom has been single for a while now. Listen, Mom, remember how you used to make us write those lists when we were younger? I think you might need to take heed to your own wisdom," India said.

"What lists are you referring to, girl? I asked.

"Oh, no, not the infamous lists. I used to hate writing those," Shea said.

"Yeah, me too, but now, I swear by them. They work. The goal list, the write-the-vision, make-it-plain lists. Remember, how you always said you have to write it out and see it on paper to hold yourself to whatever it was that you wanted. You said, if you saw it you would reach it. So, all I'm saying to you is maybe you need to take some time to yourself and figure out what it is you want in your next relationship. Write it down—everything, from the type of man you want, your boundaries—so you know up front what you're looking for so you're not confused when the next one comes along. What...don't look at me like that, you taught us well. Just look at it this way, I'm just reminding you of what you already knew, but forgot to apply it. It really works. Mom, it's okay to take advice from your daughter, especially when it was your good advice to begin with," India said.

"I guess you got me there, young lady. You're right, that's exactly what I should do. Now, I'm worn out. Let's go to bed, ladies. I can't hang like I used to," I said before kissing them both good night.

Chapter Sixteen

MONDAY MORNING HAD COME SO suddenly or it seemed. It was already time to get my daughters back to DFW so they wouldn't miss their flight. I was already anticipating their next visit. Maybe the next time, it would be all of them, Zach too. But somehow, I knew that wasn't going to happen—at least no time soon. For whatever reason, Zach always seemed to have other things on his agenda. When I'd asked him about it, he'd made up the excuse he had just gotten a new position and couldn't take the time off. I didn't know the real reason, so I left it alone.

What I wasn't going to do any longer was blame myself for how anyone felt or believed their life's outcome should have been based on my doing the best I did for them as a parent. I had that enlightenment some years back after I had been fortunate to meet a young man named Niles who spoke at a youth rally at my church who shared his life story with me. Based on Niles upbringing, he had come from a broken family—both parents in and out of the penal system—and was raised by his single grandmother. It broke my heart when he shared how he longed for a parent to show up at his basketball and football homecoming games, that the most crucial thing he remembered was not having anyone to give a rose to, how that made him feel. Imagine the loneliness and abandonment he must have felt. Now Niles is one of my church's mentors to young men. He turned out to be a law-abiding citizen and hardworking individual, yet he had been dealt a much harder hand than any of my children could ever have imagined.

I was drawn to his story because at one time, I too suffered shame and embarrassment as it related to how I was raised. But the takeaway is this: You don't have to be what you're from. You can choose not to be the way you were raised. Niles shared his story, and it was heartwarming. You just never know what a person has gone through and what has made them into who they are. I had always tried to surround Zach with positive male role models when he was younger. Even with that, sometimes children strayed and made bad choices. Not that I was naïve, but I was completely oblivious to the plight many black boys faced as a result of a missing father and sometimes mother in their household because I was there for mine. I listened to his story, and it changed my outlook on raising boys specifically. I learned boys tend to act out behaviorally rather than vocally when they are going through trauma. I was glad to know that eventually it turned out well for Niles and he was giving back to his community by being a mentor and role model for young black children. I had no regrets. Like I said, I did the best I could with what I had.

After I let India and Shea off at their departure gate, I headed out the south exit of DFW to resume my life. I had plans to stop by the gym then go out to see Maysa, Isla, and Mona for our weekly staff meeting. My music was blasting, I listened to Mary J. Blige's *The Strength of a Woman*. I guess I was feeling encouraged and a need to empower myself. My song was interrupted with a no ID call. I couldn't believe what I was seeing. What timing. Not while I'm driving, I thought. This can't possibly be. Is this the call I've been waiting for?

"Hello," I answered.

"Hey. How've you been? I'm surprised I caught you," Clayton said.

"Really? Oh, I'm fine. What can I do for you, Clayton?" I answered.

"Oh, I was just calling to see how you were. I've been calling and texting, but I guess you were too busy to see that. Then I went out of town for a few weeks. I'm just getting back in town, so I thought I'd give you a call. You must have answered by mistake."

"Oh no, as a matter of fact, I was hoping I'd hear from you again. You say you've been out of town. So did you go alone, or were you with Christy? You see, a little birdy dropped a piece of information in my lap a while ago that your wife's name is Christy. You live on Glendale Heights Road in Tolliver, Texas. When were you going to tell me about that, Mr. Clayton? Is

Christy enjoying your single life as much as you are? How dare you insult my intelligence, and you have the egregious gall to call me as if you aren't married. What makes you think I would even entertain your foul ass knowing you're married? I'm outraged and appalled that you disrespected my boundaries. Unless you want me to inform Christy of your indiscretions, I suggest you lose my number and never use it again. You got that, playa," I said.

"No problem. I just thought I'd give you a call. I guess I'd better get going. You have a good one," Clayton said and hung up so fast I thought I had imagined the entire phone call.

The nerve of that man. Dirty bastard interrupted my vibe. I resumed listening to Mary and drove on. This time "Thick of It" played.

Chapter Seventeen

AFTER I FINISHED MY WORKOUT at the gym, I showered, put on a change of clothes, and headed out to Diva's. I wanted to tell Maysa about Clayton and also wanted to hear if any new developments had occurred with the Olivia situation.

When I got there, Maysa, Isla, and Mona were already seated in the back office they used as a conference room. I had been told the meeting would be to go over the financial statements for the month and other information regarding the businesses. So far, it sounded like business was good. Profit was made, so there was no cause for worry. I liked that the girls were openminded and weren't opposed to other business opportunities that related to the beauty industry. One idea in particular was they were brainstorming other avenues such as online classes and training. They were trying to figure out the teacher licenses, legalities, and other how-tos and so forth. These girls had good heads on their shoulders. All in all, it was a good meeting, and again, I was glad to have become acquainted with them.

Maysa and I drifted off upstairs to her salon afterward. I ran it all down, my convo with Mr. Clayton.

"Girl, no he didn't call after all this time. Some men have all the nerve, don't they?" Maysa asked.

"Absolutely do, but I'm still tripping about how fast he got off the phone. I barely had time to say all of what I wanted to say to his ass," I said.

"I know, right? That dirty—" Maysa said, as I cut her off in mid sentence.

"Don't even say it. I done said it so many times already, the dirty bastard," I said.

By the time we were done talking, Maysa and I have finished a bottle of pinot grigio. She looked at her phone as if she just remembered something.

"Girl, I forgot today is Todd's birthday. I guess I should call him and tell him Happy Birthday, huh?" Maysa said.

"Well, I mean, I guess so. That's your boo, isn't it? You mean you don't have plans to be with him tonight on his birthday? What's up with that, or maybe you guys are celebrating this weekend," I said as I took another sip of my near empty glass.

"We're not exactly in a good space right now. Truth be told, we haven't been in a good space for quite some time. I've just not said anything about it," Maysa said.

"You want to talk about it?" I asked.

"Naw, not really. He's an idiot. Same old stuff, you know what I mean, and I'm just tired of it. Everything always has to be his way or the highway. Well, I guess I'm headed south on Interstate 35 East ' cause I'm not gonna let him do me. He thinks 'cause he buys nice gifts and stuff like that, he can talk to me reckless. Well, guess what? I ain't having it," Maysa said.

"Well, I'll say this much without getting in your business: If respect isn't being served at the table, stop showing up for dinner, you feel me? That's all I'mma say," I said.

"Girl, shut yo' mouth. You ain't said nothing but a word. I already know. Honestly, we're done. It's a matter that neither one of us has finally admitted it. All we do is argue," Maysa said.

"I don't know what kind of a relationship that is... When you wake up, you'll know, and I put emphasis on when 'cause hopefully you don't walk through this life asleep and in darkness forever. Won't nobody have to tell you. But hey, bae, I'm no relationship counselor, but I do know respect. We women have to demand it. Men don't have a problem letting us know what they want, will or won't deal with, hell...by the same token, we have to let them know too. It's called boundaries. Confident women set healthy boundaries. Better yet, ask yourself, do you even know what yours are? We have to first know what our boundaries are. That way, you won't allow certain treatment because you know your value. If you don't know, you won't be in nothing but a mess. You see, for years, we've been told the law of attraction is opposites attract. Hell naw, that's wrong. The law of attraction is like attracts like. You don't have to raise a thousand dollars' worth of hell to let a man know what you will or won't put up with. Stand your ground. You have to prioritize your needs ahead of time, know who you are, know what you're worth, and if he isn't willing to be that then accept it's not a good fit and move on," I said.

"Girl, you crazy, but I know you're right. This wine got you philosophizing, okaaay," Maysa said.

"I'm just saying, a lot of times, after a breakup or what-not, we tend to retreat and over-analyze the breakup by asking ourselves what we did wrong, what could we have done better when hell you didn't do a damn thing wrong. It was simply it was a bad fit. Men can't give you what they don't have the capacity to give. You're good if that particular person didn't see the value in you, then it's okay. It doesn't mean you're bad or he's bad, it simply means you aren't compatible. Ain't nothing wrong with you. Let it go, sista. It took me a long, long time to realize this, but I get it now. And guess what, you'll find joy and comfort in knowing how to be selective in your future choices. You won't be so quick to jump at the first man slanging his dick your way 'cause what you want is worth way more than that," I said.

I was relieved to have made it home and in one piece from Maysa and the girls' place, I ended up having a Starbucks coffee on the drive home, and luckily for me, I used the bathroom before I left because traffic on the freeway was horrendous. I drank that wine too fast, and I knew it. Over the next few days, I reminisced about my daughters' visit. They had texted me after their arrival home to let me know there were no flight delays and they had made it back safely. I was back to my regular routine.

Me, Harmony, Connie, and Suni had decided to have our conference call on Sunday to discuss the plans for our trip. Today, was Thursday, and I was already over the hump day back into the swing of things at home, the gym, and at the shop.

I hadn't bothered to tell Maysa about the call from Lance because I was still trying to sort it out. But I definitely had made a physical note to discuss it with my girls on Sunday. Ever since Lance's phone call, I had been doing some self-evaluation in terms of whether or not there were any males from my past I needed to apologize to, or better yet make amends with. Right off the bat, I couldn't think of any, but I knew if I had given it more thought, I could come up with someone, especially knowing I hadn't exactly been a saint back in the day. My failure to communicate my feelings in my previous relationships typically resulted in some form of cheating as a way of getting back at someone. Go figure. I wonder who I really hurt as a result of that, them or me.

I didn't know if it was an age thing or what, but lately I had been doing a lot of thinking about self-discovery and the process of evolving, mine in particular. My intent was to become a better person, and with that came intentional acts by me to ensure I accomplished it. I mentally replayed over and over what India said about me not wanting anyone in my life, about Lance saying I was intimidating, my previous blame-shame, and how to process it all. Was I too independent? Was I giving off the impression I could do it all by myself? Well damn, sounds like I'm being penalized because I'm ambitious, wanted more in life, educated, and worked hard to achieve and maintain it. There's got to be some sort of balance here. Before I reached for my new journal, I was looking through old ones and saw a passage dated November 4, 2004 , there I had written my thoughts about trying to be a better person, blame, blah, blah, blah.

"You know what, I'm done with this repetitive bullshit. Seems all my life I've been singing the same old song. I'm once and for all burying this crap, and I've decided I'm not carrying this baggage another step farther," I looked up from the passages and said aloud.

Then I began to journal my enlightening moment, a profound rite of passage, a commitment to myself. I jotted down, "I'll live purposefully with intention to practice gratitude where I am. I will live in the flow of my life and what's right for me. The time is now, and I deserve it.

Chapter Eighteen

HARMONY, SUNI, CONNIE, AND I GOT on our conference call. It was Sunday night around seven-ish. I dialed in using the new Zoom video conferencing line per the invite Connie had sent us. Connie had always been the one who was computer savvy and enlightened us on the latest and greatest gadgets as related to technology. So tonight, instead of us using the free conferencing call line, she thought she'd get us up and running with the times, stating she needed to see us and our expressions when she gave us the information about our upcoming trip to Africa. Yes, I said Africa, not Jamaica as we had previously discussed. Somewhere along the line, Connie felt we needed to visit the Motherland, so she put together what she deemed a great opportunity for us to do so.

I will admit, it's been my desire to visit Victoria Falls in Zimbabwe ever since I   witnessed the pictures of an elderly vacationer during our Martha's Vineyard trip. The pictures were the opulence of a world of wonders. The appearance of Victoria Falls was a sight to behold. I believe it encompasses the largest waterfalls in the world. I can only imagine the peace and tranquility of its beauty. I recalled from a class Africa is made up of over fifty countries, so I was curious to hear what Connie had in mind. I promised myself to be optimistic and open minded about the trip and didn't want to come across as being too controlling as I have been in the past, especially now since I'd committed to work on myself. Besides, I loved our vacationing together. The rewards of traveling were limitless. It gave us a chance to reconnect, rekindle with one another, and most importantly, to see other parts of the world and in some cases see how other folks lived. I always said it paid to visit other places. It definitely broadens your perspective and horizon. Yes, it does.

"Good evening, ladies. Okay. Hey, I see you, Harm, and Bria. I just got the notification Suni is joining so I'll let her in, I always set these virtual meetings up using a waiting room, don't ask me why. I'm so proud of you girls. Look at y'all being all high tech and stuff," Connie said.

This Zoom thing was definitely a new experience for us alright. Leave it to Connie who always had to do the most as the youth say today. I just got used to using Skype and FaceTime, now Zoom. What the heck? Connie had sent us an email with detailed instructions on setting up the video conferencing service along with the details and itinerary for Africa.

"Alrighty then. Looks like we're all here…there. I see you all now. Can everyone see me and everyone else? If not, slide your phone screen over if you're using your phone, otherwise if you're on your laptop, you can adjust the view at the top right. Harm, you're on mute. Make sure you guys are unmuted. This is so cool, I just love it," Connie said, amused.

"Girl, we could have FaceTimed. You know we just learned how to do that," I said.

"Naw. Y'all coulda FaceTimed. You know I don't have an iPhone," Harmony said.

"Your ass needs to get with the program, Harm," Suni said, laughing.

"Nope. My Android serves me well, and it takes the best pictures," Harmony said.

"So, I only scheduled this call for the first free forty minutes, girls, so let's get down to business. I hope by now, you've all had a chance to look at the information I sent. Any questions? I tried to get us the best price for flights and resorts, transportation to attractions that are listed and so forth. Y'all know I don't want to hear Bri's mouth about our resort accommodations," Connie said.

"Girl, I haven't said one word. I did my research. They all look decent so far. I just want to be safe, have a wonderful experience, and get back home alive," I said.

"Yes, we all do, crazy lady," Connie said.

"A damn fool," Harmony said, and we can see her shaking her head.

"Whatever. I just said what y'all were thinking," I responded.

"Are the attractions within walking distance from the resort and will we have to pay for attractions not covered on the list? Suni asked.

"Walking distance? Girl, this ain't New York. We aren't doing any outside walking in South Africa unless it's on our resort ," I chimed in before I knew it.

"I know that's right," Harmony said.

"That's a good question, if there are attractions we want to visit that are not on our prepared itinerary we will have to pay extra. Well, when we take our excursions, safaris or what-not, depending on what we choose to do, the cost of transportation will be arranged ahead of time based on where we go and what we want to see so there are no surprises regarding additional costs. But back to your question, Suni, there's nothing within walking distance of our resort. It's all inclusive with three meals. Also, you saw I chose three resorts so we can vote on which one. Just send me a text with your pick. I listed round-trip airfare per person based on each of our departure airports. Keep in mind, I chose September 18 through the 26 rates, which are subject to change based on our actual reservation. Are the dates good for everyone?" Connie asked.

"Oh, I have one more question: Have you married ladies discussed the timeframe with your husbands? I don't want them thinking me and Suni picked this duration. You two always get us in trouble, especially you, Connie, when you know most of these ideas are yours, just like the butterflies. You had the men thinking I spearheaded getting those tattoos. Assure me Chad and Jamal are on board with these travel plans, please," I said.

"That's a good point," Suni said.

"I discussed it with Chad, and he's good with it. He said he doesn't ever want to be on a plane for that length of time, and he understands going that far will require an extended stay. What about Jamal, Harm?" Connie asked.

"Jamal is good with it too. His biggest concern of course is our safety. He's already researching what we need to do to protect ourselves while abroad. But otherwise, the timeframe is no issue with him. In fact, he agreed to pay for my trip as an early birthday gift," Harmony replied.

"Whoa, that's what I'm talking 'bout. You know you have the best husband," Suni said.

"Yes, he's definitely a keeper. He's a great person all the way around. So considerate, thoughtful, and kind. Always doting on you, You should feel so blessed, Harm. I'm so happy for you. Chad's a good man, too, Connie. You know how spoiled you are," I joked. But each one knew I was sincere. Both Connie and Harmony had really great relationships with their spouses. Jamal and Chad had proven to us ladies over time what it meant to be good male role models to each of their families.

Everyone agreed on the dates and said they would send Connie a text regarding which resort they liked. We also said we needed to have another call next Sunday evening so we could catch up on our basic girl talk. I for one, was interested in an update from Suni about her breast surgery, and we didn't have the opportunity to hear whether Connie and Chad moved his mom in. Since we only had forty minutes on the free Zoom call, we wrapped it up and ended our session. I don't know why Connie didn't just pay for the additional time. I kept my thoughts to myself though. Hell, had I been thinking we all could have just called back in to get an additional forty minutes. Oh well, when you're our age you don't think like you used to.

Chapter Nineteen

"HEY, MA. HOW'VE YOU BEEN?" Zach asked.

"I'm good, son. How are you? So good hearing from you. I thought you had forgotten about me," I responded in my phone.

"You're so funny. Naw, I've been so busy. Before you say it, never too busy for you. I talked to the girls. Sounds like y'all really had a good time together. I was glad to hear that," Zach said.

"Yes, a good time was had by all. I can't wait for us all to be together for Thanksgiving. That will be a good time, too, I'm sure. So, what's up with you, son? Have you been staying out of trouble?" I asked.

"Who me? You know I don't get into no trouble; I keep a very low profile. I just go to work, smoke a little, have my drink at home, and chill. That's pretty much it for me. I'm not out here in these streets," Zach said.

"Good. Keep it that way. How's your significant other these days? I would call a name, but it's hard for me to keep up."

"*Awww,* now there you go. I'm not seeing anyone these days. I've been too busy working, but I wanted to give you a call to let you know I was thinking about you and I can't wait to have some of your peas and cornbread for Thanksgiving. And the dressing, candied sweet potatoes, mac and cheese, greens, potato salad, the cakes... Man, I miss your cooking," Zach said.

"What? Is that all you miss, fella?" I laughed.

"Naw. I'm just saying... I miss you too. I can't wait to get together for the holidays though. You know how we do," Zach said.

"Yep, and I can't wait for us all to be together for the holiday. I'm glad you called. That was very sweet of you to think of your dear old momma. Anything else on your mind that you'd like to talk about, honey?" I asked.

"Nope. I'm all good. I just wanted to hear your voice. I guess you don't know how good you got it 'til things change. Let me say this while I'm thinking about it. Ma, I really appreciate how you instilled the holidays and our family traditions. You always made a big deal out of them and pulled us all together. I know a lot of my homies didn't do nearly the things we did as a family, so I just wanted to say thanks, and that's one of the many things that I love about you," Zach said.

"*Awww.* ffj anks, honey. It was my pleasure. I guess it came natural to me because I grew up so alone at times during the holidays, so I wanted it to be the extreme opposite for my family.

You guys didn't know the strings I pulled to make it happen, but that wasn't for you to know. I wouldn't redo any of it. The important thing was we were always together and had lots of good ole family fun with one another and a good meal to enjoy. The holidays and my family are everything to me—and us. So, how's work going?" I asked.

"Things have been really picking up. This promotion has not only given me more responsibility but more income. Just so you know, I've been working on getting my finances in order and paying off some debt. That's one reason I've been working so hard lately. Thanks for instilling that in us, too, Ma. Now I see how important it is to have a budget, good credit, and such in check. I'm trying to build wealth. Like you always say, I want to be the lender and not the borrower," Zach said.

"Wow. I guess you were listening. Well, praise the Lord. Yep, you're right. It pays to have your financial health in order, that's for sure. A lot of what I know I had to learn by trial and error. It doesn't matter if you've made a mistake in the past, just pick yourself up and decide to change it. When you make a decision, you're committing to change, which then leads to a plan of execution so you reach your goal. You know how I get; I didn't mean to get on my soapbox, but you started it. Anyhow, I'm happy to know you're working toward your financial goals and things are looking up for you."

"Absolutely am. The more money I free up, the more I'll have to invest. At the rate I'm headed, I'll have a nice nest egg for my retirement. I don't want to work hard for the rest of my life. But anyhow, I'mma let you get back at what you were doing. I'll holla at you again soon. Love you."

"I love you, too, honey."

It was good to hear from Zach. He didn't call that regularly, but when he did, it was impactful and meaningful. He was more present in person and not much for talking on the phone—at least not with me. With that being said, I ensured he had my full attention in the event he needed to express his inner thoughts to me. Even as an adult, my son still had his issues from time to time with the fatherless aspects of his upbringing because on occasion he mentioned it, and I wanted him to know it was okay for him to share his emotions with me. Doing so was therapeutic and helped to build his strength and character. I guess that was why he used social media as an outlet. I wondered why he hadn't pursued a career in radio or something similar as often as he seemed to enjoy trivia and getting people hyped up on social media. He could've easily succeeded as a radio personality had he chosen to be. At any rate, I understood, which is why I didn't hesitate to let him know no matter what, I would always be there for him and that he could be anything he wanted to be, regardless of who hadn't been present in his life. Some might say he was a momma's boy. I, on the other hand, would say damn what they said. He's my son, and his life was significant to me.

After my conversation with Zach, I tried journaling but was too distracted. I had decided to work on my list of folks I wanted to make amends with. I wasn't exactly sure what I was going to do with the list once I compiled it, but I knew once I put it on paper, I would then be committed to putting it behind me, releasing it, and moving on. Maybe the girls would agree to us doing some sort of pronouncement or proclamation ceremony in

Africa. I'd run it by them on our next call to see what they thought.

I heard once you visited the Motherland, you're not the same, so it seemed to me that would be the perfect place to do some sort of ritual ceremony for my amends list to set it free. The girls might even want to take part in it. My idea is to decide to change an old habit and commit to doing better. Mine was the amends. Theirs can be whatever they choose.

The next Sunday evening conference call went smoother than the last. Connie received all of our texts regarding the resort accommodations, and ironically, we all had chosen the same one, Ellerman House, a Cape Town luxury hotel and villa. Sounded like the dream vacation. Connie had even included a safari and a visit to Victoria Falls in our itinerary. But from the looks of where we would be staying, we could also relax on the expansive grounds, indulge in a spa, and simply enjoy the awesomeness of Mother Nature at its grandeur. The Ellerman House sat near the Atlantic, canvassing a breathtaking view of the ocean and incredible mountains. According to Connie and her research, spring in South Africa is September to November, so we had picked a good time to go. It was Africa. We were geared up for the heat, so it didn't matter to any of us. We were excited to go.

"I'm glad we got the biggest part of the trip figured out. Now we can complete our payments and work on getting our spending money in check. That was such a great idea for us to start our vacation fund," Connie said.

"Well, hell, I don't know about y'all, but if it wasn't for my vacation fund, there's no way in hell I would be going on vacation with y'all, and especially not to Africa," Suni said.

"Girl, all it takes is a little planning and sacrifice. You know we've talked about this before. Don't trip, Suni," I said.

"Yeah, I know we have, but our excursions keep getting bigger," Suni said.

"You only live once, and when you're dead, it's a wrap," Harmony said.

"You got that right. Suni, don't you have something to share with us? I've been trying to be patient and let you initiate the conversation, but I guess we've got to pry information out of you. When's your surgery, and will it interfere with our travel plans?" I asked.

"Well, I guess, now's as good a time as any. Hell, I can't keep anything from you. I've already started the process," Suni said.

"Process? What process?" Harmony asked.

"What did I miss? What are you talking about, Suni?" Connie asked.

"What the hell do you mean, you've already started the process? I just talked to you a few weeks ago. You led me to believe you were still in the consultation stages. So how far in the process are you?" I asked.

"Okay, okay. I think I need to get a drink first. What the hell is going on here?" Connie asked.

"Connie, you don't even damn drink. Hold up and let Suni fill y'all in," I said.

"I don't drink, but I need a drink and cigarette, weed, or something. Y'all asses are scaring me. You know I'm too old for this. What is going on?" Connie demanded.

Suni went into all the details about her breast surgery, and come to find out, she had already had the surgery, had the expanders put in, gone in and had the silicone implants and was now in the recovery phase. All in all, it had been a six-month ordeal, all of which Suni had not shared any of the actual events with us other than her spoon-feeding me that bit about her consultation and the BRCA genes and so on. Suni stated her reason had to do with not wanting to bother anyone. She said her sister and one of the elderly women from church were the ones who accompanied her to the appointments.

"So there, I'll be all good, with new tits and all by the time we travel to Africa. You girls have always been there for me, and I know it, but I knew this was going to be alright, and I just didn't want to make that big a deal out of it. Please forgive me for this one. So, if y'all are done chastising me, let's get on with the next order of business. Connie, what's the itinerary for our trip? I saw in an email our last night had an open spot ceremony to be determined. I thought this was a girls trip, so, who's getting married or remarried? I know it's not me," Suni said.

"This woman is so crazy. I just don't know about you. If you weren't recovering, I'd fly to Rockford and kick your ass myself. You know damn well it's a girls trip. Ain't nobody getting married. That wouldn't make any sense at all. But I was wondering what that was about, so spill it, Connie," Harmony said.

"Whew. My nerves are wrecked. Suni, you better make damn sure you're okay. Otherwise, you're gonna have two ass whoopin's coming. But no, it's not me either. I'll let Bria tell y'all what that's about. I think it's a cool idea though," Connie said.

"And make that three ass whoopin's. Suni, you know I ain't letting you off the hook that easy. It's not a marriage ceremony. Here's what I've got in mind: So ever since that phone call I received from Lance, it's got me to thinking, and I can't seem to get it off my mind about that whole making amends thing that Lance claimed was why he was calling. I too could benefit from releasing the weight of my own previous transgressions and making amends to some men. I mean, I want to publicly say to you, my girlfriends, that I want you to hold me accountable for my actions going forward. Understand, I realize I can't undo the past. It's already done. But what am I going to do going forward? I can do something about my actions, and one of the things I commit to doing is number one, I forgive myself for the past, for the times specifically when I cheated on my partner, whoever it was at the time, because I don't want to draw that type of bullshit into my life going forward. I am truly remorseful that I didn't know any better. I didn't communicate my feelings nor did I know what I wanted, so how could I expect any different than what I got from them?" I said.

"Whew, you scared me. Shit, I thought you wanted to go to folks and start confessing. Don't do that. Hell, it ain't too late for a man to come back and kill your ass. Confess all you want but tell us some shit you just got to take to the grave," Suni cut in and said.

"Suni will you shut the hell up, I'm trying to hear what Bri is saying. Go on finish, girl," Harmony said.

"I know that's the damn truth," Connie said.

"Leave it to Suni. But seriously, number two is, to forgive others. I will no longer hold grudges for how or what has happened to me in my past. I release that negative baggage, and I'm moving on. My last idea, I've decided to be mindful of my intentions. What I'm trying to say is old habits can be broken. I said all this to share with you ladies a plan for how we can have an outward show of this shedding of old habits or whatever you want to call it by having a rites of passage ceremony similar to a South Africa Zulu Maiden Reed ceremony. You all can research that later, but for now what I'm proposing is on a much more intimate scale with just us on our last night. Y'all know we always do some sort of theme night or something to commemorate our adventures, so why not do this? Hell, you all can come up with your own commitments to pass during the ceremony. Mine is amends. Yours can be whatever you choose, anything—like your finances, weight, and exercise, whatever... So, what do you think?" I asked.

"I just have one thing to say to you, Bri, I believe the Lord knows your heart and has already forgiven you for any and all things you've already repented in your life. None of us are perfect. You are loved and are loveable, so don't go changing a bunch of shit for nobody. We love you just the way you are. Ain't nothing wrong with you or us for that matter, but I get it. Sounds like an okay idea, if that's what you really want to do. I'm in. I just had to say that much," Connie said.

"*Awww,* that's so sweet, Connie, but no, this is something I want to do as a way of holding myself accountable. Let me be honest: Y'all know I read a lot of self-help books. I guess the icing on the cake was Lance's phone call was like a confirmation to me because I had just finished reading this book by A. R. Bernard, Four Things Women Want from a Man. I tell you that book changed my life. Besides the Bible, the principle knowledge in this book really impacted my life in ways you ladies wouldn't imagine. With that being said, I've made a conscience decision to live differently as if my life depended on it, 'cause actually it does. So yeah, it's what I want to do," I said in response to Connie.

Harmony thought my idea sounded good, as long as I wasn't trying to assume blame for my past but only my role in what had occurred in past relationships. Zuni was outnumbered and agreed to the idea as well and even went as far as to say there were some things she could improve on, one was her use of so much profanity. We all laughed because we had heard that before.

I further explained I wanted to change the narrative of my past where I went from relationship to relationship without taking time to get to know myself and what I wanted. Like I've always stated, I wasn't exactly an angel in my past relationships. There were some things I could have done differently. For one, I could have communicated better, but instead, my first line of defense was self-preservation—which unfortunately was why I and so many others like me have cheated on our significant others. Whew, such a lack of integrity, we chose to go outside our relationships hoping to get some lacking fulfillment. But that was wrong on so many levels. I can't undo what's been done, but I can start with a clean slate going forward. I want to proclaim no more. I had decided also I needed to prepare myself for my next relationship. I was open to love, and yes, I wanted companionship, but in order to be really ready, there were some things I needed to come face-to-face with first. I couldn't expect anyone to give me what I wasn't willing to give. It goes back to the law of attraction—like attracts like—and if that's true, then what I want from a man, I'll be to a man.

The ceremony would be an outward show of my burying my past transgressions, making amends, and moving on. Sharing the experience with my girlfriends was something I felt in my heart of hearts needed to be done in order for me to make way for what was to come ahead. I had always heard if you know better, you do better.

The girls all agreed to our doing the rites of passage/ proclamation ceremony our last night in Africa. Each one stated she would work on her own list. We agreed not to make it mandatory to share our lists, but we would bring them on the trip in decanters and release them in the Atlantic Ocean. We would work out the particulars later. For now, we were on ready, set, go.

After the call, I attempted to get back to journaling but was so overcome with emotion thinking about Suni and all she had been through. Lord sure knows who to pick for various roles in life. Suni is strong to have gone through so much. My mind also drifted to Maysa. I realized it had been a while since I last spoke with her. I glanced over at my phone to see the time. Maysa was a night owl. It was eleven-fifteen. She might still be up. I picked up the phone, scrolled to her name, and tapped.

"Girl, when I tell you I was just thinking about you, I kid you not. How you doing? Is everything alright?" Maysa asked.

"Yeah, girl, I'm fine. I just got off my conference call with the girlfriends, and I realized I hadn't touched base with you in a couple days. I'm sorry to call so late,   but I knew you might be up. I was only gonna let it ring a couple times. What's going on?" I asked.

"Well, I guess my cousin Steph's got more problems than I thought. How about the police were called to investigate a matter of one of those foster girls that she's keeping at her house? They're saying that creep of a man   of hers has gotten the girl pregnant," Maysa said.

"What? Are you serious? That's awful," I said.

"Yeah. I guess the girl told one of Olivia's friends who's cousins with the girl. From what the girl said, Steph knew all along that something was going on, but she's been trying to cover for him," Maysa said.

"She's crazy, that's all I've got to say about that. What's her deal? What would make her want to put up with that creep? I guess you don't have to worry about your uncle Juke or nobody else handling that business for you 'cause that punk is going to be in jail and rightfully so. Your cousin Stephanie needs to get her head out the sand. She needs some therapy," I said.

"Yeah, she does. I wonder if something happened to her in the past that has made her believe that's how she should be treated. It sure makes me wonder. But I'm not gonna worry about it too much 'cause I could care less about what happens to him, and I can't worry about a grown woman who chooses not to do better for herself," Maysa said.

"Didn't you tell me she was real active in church and all? I hate to say it, but sometimes those are the worst ones. They use

Christianity as an excuse for acceptance of all sorts of inexcusable behavior. Women like that will stay in unworthy relationships for eternity when at the end of the day, all it is has to do with is their lack of self-worth. You teach people how to treat you. The Lord ain't in that nowhere," I said.

"Yeah, every time the church doors open, she's in there fanning around, all dressed up, and him too. They're going to bust hell wide open, that's what they're gonna do. Hypocrites, straight hypocrites," Maysa said.

"How is Olivia?" I asked.

"She's good. Oh, and Uncle Juke had already intervened before we got the word about this latest incident. I just told him I didn't want any details, but I bet we won't have any more problems from Steph's trifling man," Maysa said.

"Girl, I know. Some details we don't need to know, especially as it relates to that. Okay, other than that, how are things with you and Todd? Are you still seeing him, sounded like you were about to break up with him but I thought I'd ask about him anyhow 'cause I didn't know if you were serious or just fed up at the moment. I would've thought you two would have spent the weekend together or something. You're always working, May. When do you make time for him?" I asked.

"I know, that's the one thing I hate about me, I'm so indecisive about him. We spent some time together on Saturday afternoon. We went to the Bishop Arts District and walked around. We grabbed something to eat at a pizza joint and had dessert at a spot. I will admit it was nice. We didn't argue at all, but that's because I was too tired for his shenanigans so I just rolled with the flow," Maysa said.

"You are so funny, May. What is it that you're looking for? Do you even know? I've had three serious relationships in my lifetime so far, and it's taken me up until now, not being involved seriously with anyone for the past two to three years for me to be clear about what I truly want out of a relationship. Have you given it some thought? I mean, do you have clarity about what you want?"

"Yeah, I've thought about it. One of the things I want is to be married, and he's made it plain that's not where he's headed," Maysa said.

"Well, have you considered the gift of goodbye? Clearly, you both are not on the same page. Or is it that you think he'll change his mind? What is it? And what's with the urgency to get married? Trust me, it can be overrated when done with the wrong person. I've been there done that two times, so just be sure that's what you're ready for. Don't get me wrong, I think marriage is a beautiful institution, one that hopefully I'll see again in my lifetime, but honestly, I know there's some things I need to work on before I traipse down that aisle again. I'm just talking about me though," I said.

"Yeah, I've given it a lot of thought. I'll be forty-four next year. I've already accepted that I'll never have a child of my own, but I know I want to be somebody's wife. I think I deserve that happiness, don't you? I mean look at you, Ms. Bria, you're a good woman. You deserve to be loved too," Maysa said.

"Oh, okay. So I get it. You have this expectation that just because your biological timeclock is running out you should be married by a certain date. Is that it? And as for me, trust me, I'm fine. I know I'm a good catch, but I'm not quite ready to be caught. Like I said, I still have some work to do. You can say I'm getting prepared, and when it happens, I'll be ready. But back to you, don't let other folks' life expectations deem what and when the timing is right or should be for you. Just be grateful for where you are. You'll be surprised at how happiness will begin to pour into your life in every aspect, including the right man coming along. It also doesn't mean something's wrong with you or Todd. It could just mean your timing is off. I'm not trying to give a wealth of advice. Hell, sometimes I don't even know myself from day to day, but one thing I do know is I'm not going to be in any unhappy situation when I can choose to do otherwise. I'm grateful for my life and where I am right now. Honey, gratitude changes your attitude and propels your altitude. Just let that soak, that's all I'm saying."

"Well damn. Okay, that's heavy. You sure you don't have a calling on your life?" Maysa joked.

"No, I don't, trust me. If I did, you would be one of the first to know. Why don't you come to church with me next Sunday? I think you'd like my pastor. Give it some thought, okay?" I said.

"Girl, you crazy. Yes, you do have a calling. I'll talk to you tomorrow. I'm going to sleep. Bye, and good night," Maysa said.

"Whatever, Maysa. But think about what I said. Start putting yourself first. The rest will come. I mean really, putting yourself first, like your life depends on it, 'cause it does. You see, when you do that you won't have time to focus on Todd's bullshit. You'll start to attract the positive forces from the universe that will propel you into the woman you were created for. In other words, search your inner soul and know when the timing is right. Embrace it, learn from it, and move on. You might ask how do I do that. Well, you get away from all the noise in your life, cut the drama, stop trying to force the trajectory of your life, move in the flow of the present, then and only then will you hear a voice comforting you and directing you as to which path you should take. I know it sounds deep, but it's really not. You'll have much more peace. I love you, girl. I wouldn't tell you anything I didn't have to learn myself. It's a process. Don't ignore the signs."

Chapter Twenty

I MUST HAVE BEEN DREAMING I was coming through a dark tunnel trying to find my way through a fog. I kept hearing a ringing. I was wondering who was ringing the bell so loud. I couldn't figure out in which the direction the sound was coming. I kept trying to ignore it and see my way through the fog, but the noise kept getting louder and louder and longer and longer. When I found myself coming to, I realized my phone had been sounding off. I looked over to see the time. It was 11:15 p.m. My phone was ringing, I was getting a Facebook Messenger call. It was from Ava-Raye, one of Shea's cousins.

Immediately, my heart sank. I was afraid to accept the call, but with panic and hesitation, I answered.

"What's going on? Is everything okay with Shea?" I asked.

"Auntie, it's Uncle Rad. He's dead," said Ava-Raye's voice on the other end of the phone.

I immediately sat straight up in my bed. I knew it would be insidious for anyone to play a joke as harmful as what I had heard about Shea's father, but still my response was, "Are you kidding me?"

"I'm sorry, Auntie. It's true. Shea is with me. We went to check on him and found him unconscious. I've already called India and Zach. They're on their way here now. We're waiting for the coroner," Ava-Raye said.

"Oh my God. I'm on my way," I said.

I WAS ABLE TO CATCH A flight out of DFW that night. Thank God I had a few points on my American Express card, and it didn't cost me an arm and a leg, although it wouldn't have mattered if it had. Nothing—I mean nothing—was going to keep me from getting to my baby girl that night. I had reached out to Zach and India to be sure they were there for Shea just like Ava-Raye had informed me. I caught my flight, rented a vehicle, and drove from O'Hare to Rockford, which seemed like eternity. God knew best. It actually gave me an opportunity to pull myself together before I got to Shea.

The next few days were like a blur and ones I'll never forget. When I got to Shea, she was distraught. The screams I heard from her were deathly, intense, and formidable. I didn't think we'd ever get her quieted. All I kept hearing her say was "My daddy's gone, Ma. He's gone."

My heart ached for her, but this time, there was nothing I could do to fix it for her. I grabbed her and embraced her as tight as I could without saying a word. Only time would heal the brokenness and despair she was going through.

We got through it. Shea and her other siblings—Rad's other children—took care of all the arrangements. It was nice to see them all come together on one accord. I always had a hard time looking at my children as adults, but I was proud of the grown-ups each one had become, especially now, as I witnessed all of what Shea had been through. I'm sure Rad would have been proud as well with the dignity and honor in which they showed him his last rites.

I stayed in Rockford for about seven days before I decided I had done all I could do. I was assured by Zach and India, Shea was in good hands, and before I left, I was confident Shea was well capable of managing on her own. Besides, Shea and I had a good one-on-one prior to my leaving. She let me know that somehow she had mentally prepared herself for this time and for me not to worry about her. She asked that I not continue to ask how she was doing because that made her a bit melancholy, but for me to allow her space to grieve her dad's death appropriately. It would take some time. I understood that, and I let her know she could depend on me to be there for her if she needed me.

As a parent, you never get over that instinct to want to nurture your children, but you do have to allow them to sustain life on their own. I haven't ever wanted to be the kind of mother who crippled, handicapped, and enabled my children to the point they would fold under the pressures of life, so seeing firsthand how each one of them handled life's blows gave me a sense of pride and let me know I hadn't been so bad a teacher after all. I couldn't help but think how you just never know how life will turn out. Every day the Lord continues to show us signs and opportunities at greatness.

I'm so grateful Rad and I made amends years ago, so I was at peace that there were no issues of bitterness between us, and because I loved my daughter and wanted nothing more than her happiness, I was glad she and Rad had a true father/daughter relationship, which they shared for so many years. In some ways, this was added confirmation of the importance of doing what's right to people, no matter what your differences may be. As much as I had asked the question What about me? lately, I had sense enough to know it's not always about me. I'm glad I had the discernment to know when it is and when it ain't. Pardon my vernacular.

"I'm boarding now. I returned the rental, and there were no problems. Thanks for everything. I appreciate all you girls did while I was there. Just check on my babies from time to time. I know they're grown, but they're still my babies," I said to Suni over the phone. I had just arrived inside my gate in O'Hare airport.

"Girl, you know that goes without saying. I'm glad all is as well as to be expected. Shea, India, and Zach will be alright. Be sure to text when you land," Suni said.

"I will," I said.

Suni, Harmony, and Connie had shown up at the services for Rad in support of Shea. Connie and Harmony surprised us all by coming. Although it was a quick turnaround trip, and everyone had already returned to their homes, it meant a lot they thought enough of Shea and our family to come. Suni and I had a chance to spend some quality time together after the repast and during the week while I remained in Rockford. Over the years, at one time or another, we had all invested time building our friendship and being there for one another, whether it was the passing of a mother, father, sibling; a divorce; broken relationships; or whatever was important to whomever at the time. That was how we operated.

Things had happened so fast I barely had time to let Maysa know what was going on. I had finally called her a day or so prior to the service to let her know I had left town and why. Maysa being the worrier she is asked me over and over if I was sure there was nothing she could do to help, then chastised me for not calling her the night I received the news saying she would have come by and or even driven me to the airport. I got her settled down, and all was good. I knew I had found a good friend in Maysa. It was just that when I get my mind going about something that I need to get done, rather than waste time bothering folks, my adrenaline got to pumping and I didn't stop until I was in full operation mode. It's hard for me to recognize genuine assistance. That's another something I'd have to add to my list of things to work on.

It was Monday evening after I settled in, and things for me were somewhat on their way back to normal. I lit some candles to create a soothing environment and to wind down, took a bath in some essential oils and jasmine fragrance, relaxed, and soaked for a bit. Afterward, I dressed in some short silk pajamas and retreated to my bedroom, climbed in bed, and tried to calm my mind from the previous week.

Just as I was about to reach for my switch on the lamp on my nightstand next to my bed, I saw the display brighten. The messages icon was in bright green, an indication of a new text message. It was from Fav. The message read, Hey, you. Are you awake? I grabbed my glasses and pulled the phone closer to see if I had read it incorrectly. Using my thumb, I slid the screen upward to open the message to see if there was more. There wasn't.

In that instant, I went through a whole metamorphosis—rationalizing, thinking, and rethinking what could Fav possibly want and why now after so much time had passed. I hadn't heard from him in almost two year s. When I left town, I had refused to call him anymore. I had made up my mind and had moved on, and I had presumed he had too. Just thinking about him brought back fond memories of being close to him, his warm embrace, his masculine arms, his smell...

I needed to snap out of it—and quick. I was putting myself into a trance with all the visions of Fav dancing in my head. Hell, all I had received was a text. I was acting like the man was standing at my door. Look, I told myself, either you're going to text back yes, you're awake or don't respond at all and take your butt to sleep. What's so hard about that?

I'll tell you what was so hard about it. Fav just didn't know the effect he had on me. Well, I damn sure knew, and I also knew how hard it had been for me to get over him. I also knew how deep my feelings were for him, for us not to have gone any further than we had. I wasn't so sure I wanted to get sucked back into that again. It had been too hard coming back the last time. I had really lost all touch with my emotions, and I didn't want to get caught up in that scenario. So no, I wasn't responding.

"Good night, brotha. Been there, done that," I said before tossing my phone on my bed, removing my glasses, switching off my lamp, sinking beneath my covers, and laying my head on my pillows.

I tossed and turned all night.

Chapter Twenty-one

AS SOON AS I DRIFTED into that deep REM of sleep, I was jarred by the sound of my alarm on my phone. If it hadn't it been for the fact I had been awaken out of a dream about Fav, I would have thought I hadn't gotten any sleep at all. I couldn't recall the details, only that it seemed so real. I thought he was in bed with me, and I was behind him holding him as we both slept, but it was only a dream. I got up, went through my morning ritual so I could head on out to Diva's since it had been a while since I last checked in.

As I pulled up, it was about ten-fifteen. I saw Isla's car in her spot. She must have had a fitting this morning because she typically wasn't in the boutique until after eleven. Looked like a full house this morning, I thought as I looked to my right and saw Mona and Maysa's cars were parked in their designated spots as well. It was early September. Women must be getting ready for vacations, weddings, family reunions, and other fall events that required personal body care for this time of the year. I was happy to see the girls' businesses flourishing as well as they were.

I walked into the main entrance and was greeted by a young lady who had been hired as the receptionist and greeter for the spot. I said my hellos and let her know I was there to see Maysa. She picked up a phone and called to let her know I was there.

"Ms. Bria, I know you're going up to the salon, but would you be interested in any fragrance or essential oils today?" the young lady asked.

"Not now. I might check them out on my way out. Thank you," I said as I headed up the staircase. Even though I was a silent partner, most the young ladies on staff didn't treat me any different than any other client.

Maysa had a salon full—two customers were under hair dryers and one of her shampoo girls was busy shampooing another client.

"Hey, girl. I'm in the back. You can come on in here," Maysa said.

"Hey, May. How've you been?" I asked.

"Girl, it's been busy as heck in here lately, but it's all good. I'm not complaining. What about you? How's your daughter and the rest of the family? I'll bet it was hard leaving them," Maysa said.

"It was, but they're pretty strong and well capable of handling situations like these for themselves. I'm just a moment's notice away anyhow. So, fill me in: What's been going on around here?" I asked.

"Well, you know I have plenty to tell you, so why don't you go on downstairs for a spa treatment? I already paid for a session for you. I figured you could use one coming back from what you been through and all. You need some 'me' time. By the time you're done, I should be done with my clients, then we can sit and have a glass or two of wine and I can fill you in. Don't look at me like that. It's already scheduled for eleven, so go on down. They're expecting you," Maysa said.

"What? Girl, you're too much, but yeah, I definitely need it—and more than you know," I said.

I hadn't realized how tense my body was. Maysa had set me up with the works. I received the hot stone, milk, and honey body massage; a facial; and a full-body wrap. It was soothing to say the least. I had so much stress built up in my muscles, and I started to relax and feel good all over. I had an hour-and-a-half session, and afterward, I went to the sauna and sat for thirty to forty-five minutes. It wasn't often that I had the opportunity to get some quality me time, so I took advantage of my gift. It was right on time and just what I needed.

I completely lost track of time as my mind drifted to random thoughts. I focused on a form of meditation I had learned from an app that India had shared with me just to help me reach full tranquility. When I came to, I got showered, put shea butter balm all over my body, and got dressed before heading back up to see Maysa.

Looked like Maysa had cleared everyone out and had two glasses of wine sitting on one of her counters near a chaise longue.

"Girl, I'm glad you're back and everything is okay," Maysa said.

"Yeah, it's good to be back," I said. "Like I said, I knew things would be rough because of how close Shea and her dad were, but I knew she'd would be alright eventually. We just have to allow her the space to grieve. You know, unfortunately, it's just a part of life. Death is something we're all going to have to face at one time or another, whether we like it or not. We can never be prepared for it. It's just one of those things you know," I said before taking a sip of my wine.

"I hear ya, and I know what you're saying is real. So, you good, girl? You still need to take care of yourself. You good? Seems like you're a little off about something. What's going on, Ms. Bria?" Maysa said.

"I'm good, but funny you asked. Yeah, my vibe is a tad off-kilter. I received a text from an old acquaintance last night. I guess I'm still trying to figure it out," I said.

I go into detail about mine and Fav's relationship, if you will—or lack thereof.

"So, you haven't responded to his text yet? Aren't you the least bit curious about what he wants? Hell, I would've been done responded," Maysa said.

"No, I usually always respond. He texts, calls, or whatever. Doesn't ever matter how long, when, where, I've always been an available friend with benefits. No more. I'm tired of it. I'm looking for something different now, so when I get a good lead that it'll be different, I'll follow it. Until then, I'm good.

"*Hmmmph.* You say you're following his lead, huh? Well, what was that you told me about Todd when I said I was following his lead: What if he's just following your lead? Then what? Sounds like somewhere down the line, your feelings have changed for him, but he doesn't even know it. What, is he a mind reader? If he is, he must be one hell of a brother. I don't know, just seems like the rules aren't fair, you know what I mean?" Maysa asked.

"Well, that was our normal. He's never seemed bothered by not seeing me for long periods of time, so why would I think he would've cared when I told him I had retired and was relocating to Dallas? He never said don't go. As a matter of fact, hell, I don't even recall having a good farewell. It was just done," I said.

"It was done 'cause you said it. What the hell was he supposed to do? Sounds like your mind was already made up. If he's the man you say he is, he wasn't going to stand in your way. Sounds like he's confident and secure with himself, and this was y'all's normal. This is what you both became acclimated with, so how was he to know you felt any different when you hadn't mentioned it to him?" Maysa said.

"No. We're just nice to each other. We didn't have serious discussions about us per se. We were cordial with each other. We never had a disagreement, never argued. It was just nice. Like I said, when our schedules coincided, we'd see each other. Yeah, that was our normal. But toward the end, I grew tired of it, and you know, I guess I was or am ready to mean more to someone than just a friend with benefits, so I moved on," I said.

"Yeah, I get it, but the part that I don't get is you didn't give him a fair shot. You didn't let him know the game was changing. You never gave him an opportunity to say yay or nay," Maysa said.

"Yeah, whatever," I said.

"Yeah whatever alright. I know you. Does he? Does he know how hard you go when you love your man, your family, and your friends? How you cook? How you clean? Your love of art and décor in the home? How loyal you are? I think if he knew all those things about you—how deserving you are, who you are on a whole 'nother level—he'd be knocking the walls down trying to get at you. Those are good qualities. You have a lot to offer, and some man would be glad to have you," Maysa said.

"*Awww.* ffj anks, friend. ffj at's so nice of you to say those things about me. I appreciate it. I've heard it all before—from the little old ladies at church to the ladies I run into at the stores. Previous colleagues have all said the same things. Makes me wonder if something's wrong with me for being single so long this time, but really, it's not. I'm good. I just want what's for me this time and something that's real. I have to wait my turn, that's all. What's that saying, my ship will sail one day? There's a quote that says ships in the harbor are safe, but that isn't what ships are built for. In other words, it's better to get out and do the things you want to do rather than sit around and not do nothing. Meanwhile, I'm getting myself prepared to set sail, and when it's time, I'll be ready," I said.

"You're crazy. At least respond to the man's text, call his ass back, or something. What the hell is it with you? Why are you so damn stubborn? What are you afraid of?" Maysa asked.

"I don't feel like I'm running from anything. If you must know the truth, I just don't want to be hurt again. Every time I let my guard down, I'm disappointed," I said.

"You need to let that muthafucka know how you feel. I'm sorry for saying it like that, but damn. Give me your damn phone. You haven't heard from him in almost two years or better. You don't know what he wants. He can't be just calling you out the blue for no reason. Hell, if you don't want to know, I do," Maysa said, laughing.

"Girl, I'm not giving you my damn phone. Are you freakin' crazy, out of your mind? I would never allow someone else to speak for me not in my character at all," I said.

"Hell, that's it. You've been too nice. He should know by now you're not still asleep. Text him back," Maysa said.

"I am. When I get ready. Now you need to slow that adrenaline down. You're rousing up my spirt and disturbing my inner peace. I just had a much-needed spa, and here you are trying to fast forward me into another space. No, you need to relax, May. Just relax. I want what's mine. If it's meant to be, it'll be. So, bring it down, girl. Bring it waaay down. If it was important enough to him, he'll reach out again. If not, oh well. So now, what was it you had to catch me up on while I was away?" I asked as I rolled my eyes, slightly shook my head, and gestured at Maysa to bring it down. This time, I gulped a drink of wine.

"Okay, girl, 'cause you know I can be a trip." Maysa said, gulping her wine.

"I know. You do you, and let me do me. It's cool...so talk," I said.

"Yeah, well anyway, remember you had asked me to go to church with you before you left? Well, I guess that was in my spirit, so much so I decided Olivia and I would go to church on the last Sunday. The only one I could think of was Stephanie's church. I actually heard good things about the pastor, so I mean it was cool," Maysa said.

"So, was Stephanie and that man of hers there?" I asked.

"Slow down. Slow down, girl. This is my story. Just listen, just listen," Maysa said.

"Oh alright. So go on, girl," I said.

"So, we get there early, you know 'cause parking is so far away from the building and all. I would say it was about nine thirty-ish or so. My aim was to attend the ten a.m. service. They have three services—eight, ten, and noon. Okay, so we park, get into the building, and get seated. Girl, I'll bet we hadn't been seated five minutes when all of a sudden, we hear a loud commotion going on at the back of the church. We didn't know what was going on. My first thought was someone had gotten the Holy Ghost or something, then it occurred to me church hadn't even started yet. Then Olivia nudges me to look backward. Guess who it was, girl?" Maysa asked.

"Honey, I have no idea. You know I don't know many people here. Who was it? I asked.

"My cousin Stephanie and some woman done got into it at the church house, girl. I couldn't believe it. I turned around 'cause at that point, I didn't want anyone to know I knew her. All I could hear was something about, 'why you still in my face. I told you to get out my face. You done crossed the line. Your husband did. You're lying. Tell the truth, bitch.' When I tell you, it was ugly, it was a crying shame. It finally came to a head when two big burly security guards came and ushered them both out the church. Sounded like that man of Stephanie's done tore his ass again. How much more is she going to take, I don't know. Ain't no telling what type of foolishness that was about," Maysa said.

"Isn't that the truth? But in church, it must've been bad for the other woman to go off like she did. Apparently, she hadn't heard Michelle Obama's phrase, When they go low, we go high 'cause if she had—well, both of them for that matter—they should have handled that differently. Well, I'll be damn. So, you haven't heard anything from Stephanie since her life with the significant other has been unraveling? And did you say husband—so are they married or not?" I asked.

"Nope, not a word, and no, to my knowledge, they aren't married, but they're playing the role at the church house. Otherwise, he wouldn't be able to be a deacon. It's just a whole mess, that's what it is. We just have to pray for her. Hopefully, she'll wake up soon. It's one thing to deal with a trifling person privately, but publicly, that's a whole different level. Shit, either way is bad though," Maysa said.

"Definitely. Either way isn't good, and too much of somebody else's business for my plate. I'd better be on my way home. You got those heads out of here quick, didn't you, girl?" I said.

"Yes, ma'am. It doesn't take long. Most of my clients today have natural hair, so they all basically needed a good shampoo, conditioner, hot oil treatment, or twists, and done. A lot has changed with the hair industry from days past. We're not dealing with a lot of harsh chemicals like we used to, so it really doesn't take all day anymore. I'm going to get cleaned up and out of here too. Maybe I'll go down to Isla's and see if I can get some sauna time in. But you think about what we talked about. Text your man, Ms. Bria. Love you and see you tomorrow." Maysa said.

"Yeah, love you too, crazy woman," I said as we hugged each other before I left.

Chapter Twenty-two

THE WEEKS HAD GONE BY. I had gotten back into the full swing of my regular daily routine. Next week the girls and I would be leaving for our Africa trip. I was so excited and had been busy with the last of our details regarding our itinerary. It was so smart of us to join that vacation plan at our individual Credit Unions so we were sure we were covered a year or more ahead of when we needed to making our last payments. This was a major trip for us all and a large expenditure that we had been financially setting ourselves up for a long time. As time neared, our conference calls were more often during the week as we checked in regularly to ensure we had everything we needed for the trip.

A lot of our conversations included our wardrobe—what we were wearing to what event from our apparel to the type of shoes. We all decided on wearing all white to our Proclamation of Amends Ceremony, which was what we had named our last night. Africa was one of the biggest excursions we had taken together so far. To say we were a bit nervous was an understatement, but we were all very excited. We all had connecting flights from our home destinations, except for Connie, and we were set to meet up at the Charlotte Douglas airport, and from there we would catch the British Airways aircraft to Cape Town International. I had planned to leave my car at home and LYFT to the airport for convenience, which was ideal because it gave me door-to-door service.

It was the night before our departure. Alexa was playing Jill Scott Pandora Radio. I had a glass of pinot grigio while scurrying about my condo. I hadn't given any more thought to texting Fav back. Like Maysa said, I had become well adapted to our "normal." One reason was he texted so few and far in between that I had become immune to hearing from him, especially as of late because I was so busy planning for my trip along with ensuring Shea's grieving process was going well, and he just hadn't crossed my mind. Well...he actually had, but I had enough going on that I didn't focus on just him as much as I would have otherwise. I knew once I got on a mission planning and anticipating my trip, it would be that way, and Lord, was I glad my adrenaline was in high gear and my mind was productively occupied. I was longing for a life- altering experience, a transformation. Maybe I was being too deep, but something had to give, and I was open to it.

I had folded clothing and toiletries strewn every which way in my spare bedroom. My luggage laid opened on the bed, and I was somewhat packed as I attempted not to overpack. You could say I was ready to get far away from here. I subconsciously thought, Just let me get on that plane to Africa. Fav could text all he wanted, but it would be impossible to be on ready, set, go to him 'cause it wouldn't be that easy from Cape Town. Tomorrow couldn't get here fast enough.

Perhaps after our visit to the Motherland I'd know whether my expectations were too high and why I hadn't met my soul mate. Whatever. That was a fleeting thought. I'm enough. I just hadn't found the one with the right capacity to love me—all of me. So, what I'm looking for, I have to mirror. I'd already discovered that during the process of self-discovery and learning to truly love myself and committing to living my best life. The world doesn't stop, it doesn't slow down so I can achieve all my goals. No, ma'am, quite the contrary. That's why I had to be intentional about my goals, which was why we were doing the amends ceremony—I'd write it down so I could see it and so I could reach it. I heard it said, What the mind sees, it believes, then it can achieve.

I already knew I was better than I used to be. Gone were the days of feeling shame about my past, being insecure, and feeling sorry for myself. I knew my worth and my value. I was confident, consistent, and decisive, and because I knew who I was and what I'd reflected, I needed and wanted someone with a large enough capacity to love all of me unconditionally, freely— me for me. How freeing it felt to finally know my value and to understand it and know I wouldn't settle for anything less, nor did I have to bring my standards down. Yet I understood how to balance life and all that comes with it; when to show love, empathy, and compassion for others, family, friends, and loved ones; when and how to be there for them and when it's about me—Sabria (Bria) Twon.

Just as I had gotten all my belongings packed, I thought I heard a chime from my phone which was in my master bedroom. Because I had the music so loud and dancing and prancing to that Lizzo song, "Good As Hell" I wasn't sure if it was the music jamming on that Jill Scott radio or if it was in fact an alert from my phone, so I went to look and saw it was a missed call from guess who? Fav of all people. I must have thought him up. In that instant, the phone rang while I was holding it. Knowing I was about to head off to Africa in the morning, I confidently answered the call.

"Hey," I said.

"Hey you. How are you? Have you forgotten about me?" he asked.

"I'm good, and no, of course not. How could I? So what's up?" I asked.

"I was just calling to check in, making sure you're okay," he said.

"I am. In fact, I just finished packing. I'm going on my bi-annual girlfriends trip in the morning."

"Really? That sounds exciting. Where are you ladies going this time around?" he asked.

"Cape Town, South Africa," I said.

"Sounds really nice. For how long?"

"Seven days."

"Hmmm. So when you return, will you make some time for me?"

"We'll see about that when I return, my schedule is pretty full so I'll let you know.

"Oh. I'll be waiting for your return. I miss you, Bria. I know it's been almost two years, I can't stop thinking about you. You don't know how bad I have needed and wanted to speak with you, to hear your voice, I miss seeing your face. So yeah, I'll be waiting. I love you and want to be with you. That's all I want to say for now."

"What did you just say?"

Book Club Discussion Questions

1. Based on Bria's character, how was having female friendships/girlfriends significant to her growth as a woman post divorce, empty nester, and overall well-being?
2. Which character seemed to struggle the most as it related to men and relationships?
3. What character/relationship(s) did you relate to the most and why?
4. Suni made the comment, For women over fifty, everything comes to a screeching halt. How does that comment pertain to how some middle-aged women deal with the issue of dating and recognizing red flags?
5. Bria said she needed to "mirror" what she attracted. How does that comment relate to knowing who you are and setting boundaries in the law of attraction?
6. Regarding the topic predatory sexual approach to underage women, how would you handle knowing someone approached someone you knew?
7. What relevance was Bria's relationship/connection to Fav to Bria's moving forward?
8. Why do you think Bria kept Fav a secret?
9. What in your opinion was the importance of Bria wanting to make amends to her past transgressions?
10. Which of the characters seem to believe having a man was a be-all and end-all?
11. What do you think Bria's response to Fav's call will be?

About the Author

EARTHA G. GATLIN WAS BORN and reared in Rockford, Illinois. She is the author of *The Chronicles of Bria Twon*. This is Eartha's second work of fiction in the Bria Twon series. She now resides in Dallas, Texas metroplex.

www.ingramcontent.com/pod-product-compliance
Lightning Source LLC
Chambersburg PA
CBHW021156110726
47900CB00002B/600